William M'Combie Smith

Memoir of the Family of M'Combie

William M'Combie Smith

Memoir of the Family of M'Combie

ISBN/EAN: 9783337389178

Printed in Europe, USA, Canada, Australia, Japan

Cover: Foto ©Raphael Reischuk / pixelio.de

More available books at **www.hansebooks.com**

MEMOIR

OF THE

FAMILY OF M'COMBIE

" Man is properly the only object that interests man."—GOETHE.

MEMOIR

OF THE

FAMILY OF M'COMBIE

A BRANCH OF THE CLAN M'INTOSH

COMPILED FROM

HISTORY AND TRADITION

BY

WILLIAM M'COMBIE SMITH

WILLIAM BLACKWOOD AND SONS
EDINBURGH AND LONDON
MDCCCLXXXVII

PREFACE.

THE first question regarding the publication of a new book ought to be, Does it contain anything not already known to those likely to read it? Of the present work it may safely be said that much of what it contains is not already known to probable readers. The second question, in the event of the first being satisfactorily answered, ought to be, Are the contents of sufficient interest or value to warrant publication? It would be presumptuous on the part of the compiler to answer this question affirmatively. He may be permitted, however, to say, that he believes that what is authentic and historical in the life of John M'Comie of Forter is of interest

and value as illustrative of the social and political
life of the seventéenth century; and that the
record of the position attained and work accomplished by several of his descendants in Aberdeenshire, and the means by which their position
was attained and work accomplished, will be
found interesting, valuable, and instructive. If
the traditionary events are of less value, they
are still interesting, and their publication may
be excused on the ground that most of them
were likely soon otherwise to have passed irretrievably into oblivion.

W. M'C. S.

CONTENTS.

CHAPTER III.

CHAPTER IV.

CHAPTER V.

THE FAMILY OF M'COMBIE.

———•———

INTRODUCTION.

BIOGRAPHY is ever the most profitable and interesting matter for both writer and reader. The life of the most commonplace man or woman or family, it has been remarked, were it fully unfolded, would be full of interest, and in proportion as the individual or family becomes conspicuous, the interest increases. In some instances the interest attaching to a family name centres round one individual, who appears as a bright particular star, outshining all the others. In other cases the interest attaching to a family name is continued throughout many generations, by a succession of men who distinguish them-

A

selves in their day and generation as not of common mould. In either case there arises, among those inheriting the family name, that pride of ancestry so highly to be prized by those whose heritage it is. An honourable pride of ancestry is one of the most valuable incentives to the maintenance of human worth and greatness. It is from the honourable pride and ambition of the individual members of distinguished families to maintain in undiminished honour the prestige of the family name that the permanent stability and greatness of a nation arises. National pride in the nation's history, and national ambition to hand down to posterity its honour and glory untarnished, or even with added lustre, is the outcome of the combined efforts of the individuals and families comprising the nation, animated by the desire either to maintain and add to individual and family renown already acquired, or to be the first to bring renown to an individual or family not previously distinguished.

The Celtic population of the Highlands of Scotland have always been remarkable for the tenacity with which they have maintained the name and honours of the various clans, with their distinct branches or septs. This determination has naturally led to a desire to collect and preserve authentic records of the lives of the leading members of whatever clan or family has achieved an honourable position, and has through successive generations maintained that position; and the object of the present memoir is to put on record and preserve whatever has come down to the present time, through history or tradition, concerning the family of M'Combie, a branch of the Clan M'Intosh.

CHAPTER I.

ORIGIN OF THE CLAN M'INTOSH — ORIGIN OF THE FAMILY OF
M'COMBIE — CALLED CLAN M'THOMAS, ACTS OF PARLIAMENT
1587 AND 1594 — SETTLED IN GLENSHEE — INTERMARRIAGE
WITH FARQUHARSONS—BOND OF MANRENT TO LACHLAN MOR,
SIXTEENTH CHIEF OF THE M'INTOSHES.

THE founder of the Clan M'Intosh was Shaw
M'Duff, second son of the fifth Earl of
Fife, who distinguished himself in quelling a rebellion among the Moray tribes, against Malcolm
IV., about the years 1161-63, and whose descendants thenceforward assumed the name M'Intosh
= Mac-an-Toiseach = son of the foremost or chief
man. The Clan M'Intosh, of which the family
of M'Combie is a branch, was in turn a branch
of the still older Clan Chattan, the derivation of
which is uncertain. The famous fight on the
North Inch of Perth, in 1396, in the reign of

Robert III., between the Clan Chattan and Clan Quhele, was fought by the ancestors of the present M'Intoshes, M'Phersons, and Camerons.

From Angus Og, son of Angus, the sixth chief of the Clan M'Intosh, who died in 1345, were descended the M'Intoshes of Glen Tilt, who afterwards settled at Dalmunzie in Glenshee. It was probably owing to the settlement of this branch of the M'Intoshes in Glenshee, that the descendants of Adam M'William [1] of Garvamore, in Badenoch, a natural son [2] of William, [3] the seventh chief, also settled in Glenshee, Strathardle, and Glenisla.

This Adam M'Intosh, son of William, the seventh chief of the Clan M'Intosh, was the founder of that branch of the clan which afterwards came to be known by the surname of M'Thomas = son of Thomas, which in time became corrupted into M'Thomie, M'Homie, M'Omie, M'Comie, and latterly M'Combie. The surname M'Intosh was used interchangeably with M'Comie until the settlement in

[1] Appendix, Note A. [2] Appendix, Note B. [3] Appendix, Note C.

Aberdeenshire. The family of M'Combie took its rise, therefore, as a separate and distinct branch of the Clan M'Intosh in the latter half of the fourteenth century. In the original feu-charter,[1] of date 9th September 1571, the M'Combies are described as being *ab antiquo* tenants and possessors of Finnegand in Glenshee.

In the " Roll of the Landdislordis and Baillies" appended to the Act of Parliament, of date 1587, " for the quieting and keeping in obedience of the disordourit subjectis inhabitantis of the Bordouris, Hielandis, and Ilis," commonly called " The General Band," there is first given " The Roll of the names of the Landislordis and Baillies of Landis in the Hielandis and Iles, quhair brokin men hes duelt and presentlie duellis," followed by " The Roll of the Clannis [in the Hielandis and Iles] that hes Capitanes, Cheiffis, and Chiftanes quhome on thay depend, oft tymes aganis the willis of thair Landislordis : and of sum speciale personis of branchis of the saidis clannis." In

---

[1] Appendix, Note D.

the latter roll there occurs the " Clan M'Thomas in Glensche."

In the roll of the clans of 1587, following " Clan M'Thomas in Glensche," are the " Fergussonis, Spaldingis," without locality given, and the " Makintoscheis in Athoill," showing that Angus Og's descendants, together with those of Adam, son of the seventh chief, still held Glen Tilt and Glenshee as their headquarters.

In the roll of the broken clans in the Highlands and Isles, in the Act of Parliament "for punishment of thift, reiff, oppressioun, and soirning," of date 1594, there are included under "many brokin men," the "Fergussonis, Spadingis, M'Intosheis in Athoill, M'Thomas in Glensche," and "Ferquharsonis in Bra of Mar." The necessity for this second roll, so soon following on that of 1587, is set forth as follows : "Oure Soverane Lord and his estaitis in this present Parliament, considering that, nochtwithstanding the sundrie Actis maid be his Hienes, and his maist nobill progenitouris, for punischment of the authoris of thift, reiff, oppression, and sorning, and masteris and sustenaries of thevis; yet sic hes bene, and presentlie is, the barbarous cruelties and daylie heirschippis of the wickit thevis and lymmaris of the clannis and surenames following, inhabiting the Hielands and Iles," &c.

In both rolls the M'Intoshes, Fergussons, Spaldings, and M'Thomases occur together; and in the 'Geography of the Clans of Scotland,' by Mr T. B. Johnston and Colonel J. A. Robertson, the M'Intoshes are marked in the map as in Glen Tilt only, and the M'Thomas clan in the head of Glenshee, with the Fergussons lower down, and the Spaldings lowest down in what is now known as the Blackwater district, and in Strathardle around Ashintully. There is evidently something wrong in this arrangement. The M'Intoshes were in Glen Tilt previous to 1587; but they were also in Dalmunzie, in the head of Glenshee. Where the Fergussons are placed in the map, Finnegand is situated, where no Fergussons were at that time nor since; and in 1571 the M'Thomases had been "*ab antiquo*" possessors of Finnegand, and were in possession

of it for long after 1594. The Spaldings were,
until comparatively recent times, tenants and possessors in the Blackwater district of Glenshee,
and in and around Ashintully in Strathardle.
Bearing in mind that the M'Intoshes and
M'Thomases were of the same origin, and that
long after this time of 1587, or even of 1594, the
head of the Clan M'Thomas used the surname
M'Intosh interchangeably with M'Comie, there
can be little doubt but that Glen Tilt in Athole,
with the head of Glenshee, should be set down
in a clan map of the sixteenth century as held
by M'Intoshes, and the district between the head
of Glenshee and what is now the Blackwater
district, as held by the branch of the M'Intoshes
known by the surnames of M'Intosh, M'Thomas,
and M'Comie, and below the M'Comies, the
Spaldings. The Fergussons in the map ought
to be placed in the Glenshee south of Dunkeld,
held, in part at least, by Fergusson, Baron of
Fandowie, and not in the Glenshee north of
Dunkeld.

It is clearly established, however, both by the

parliamentary records of Scotland and by charter, that the M'Comies were a distinct family,
settled in Glenshee in the sixteenth century.
The phrase *ab antiquo*, in the charter of 1571,
establishes a settlement long previous to that;
and their descent from William, seventh chief of
the M'Intoshes, points to this settlement as being
probably in the end of the fourteenth or beginning of the fifteenth century.

In the roll of 1594, the M'Thomases in Glenshee are immediately followed by the Farquharsons in Braemar. The great hero of the Farquharsons was the renowned Finla Mor. In
1547, he was standard-bearer in the disastrous
battle of Pinkie, where he was slain. It is an
interesting fact that the great hero of the
M'Comies, *the* M'Comie Mor, was a lineal descendant of Finla Mor's. Finla Mor's first wife
was a daughter of Baron Reid of Kincardine-
Stewart. Their eldest son, William, married Bea-
trix Gordon, daughter of Lord Sutherland, whose
daughter was married to Thomas M'Intosh of
Finnegand. The family, therefore, had acquired

considerable influence and power in the sixteenth century; and in the words of the Act of Parliament of 1587, was depending on its own chief, "ofttimes against the will," it may be, of its feudal superior, the Earl of Athole. The concern expressed by Parliament in the doings of these "brokin men"—that is, branches of original clans who had assumed independence—naturally led these to confederate themselves. The measures adopted by the Scottish Government after the Act of Parliament of 1587, had evidently been ineffectual in bringing these broken men into submission; but the subject being taken up again so soon after, showed both that the independent branches were proving troublesome to their landlords and the Government, and that the latter was determined to bring them to account.

Accordingly, in the year following the Act of 1594, we find the distant colonies of the clan in Aberdeenshire and Perthshire granting a heritable band of manrent, at Invercauld, to Lachlan Mor, the sixteenth chief of the M'Intoshes. In this band, dated March 1595, James M'Intosh of

Gask, Donald Farquharson of Tulligarmont, John Farquharson of Invercauld, George, Lachlan, and Finlay Farquharson, brothers to the laird Donald (these four were sons, and John of Invercauld a grandson, of Finla Mor), Duncan M'Intosh of Dalmunzie, and Robert M'Homie in the burn of Glenshee, promise to maintain, fortify, and defend Lachlan and his heirs, "as our naturall cheiff."

CHAPTER II.

FROM the end of the sixteenth to about the middle of the seventeenth century, there seems to have been a period of comparative quietude. The tranquillity of the rest of the country, from the Union of the Crowns to the beginning of the great Civil War, exerted its

influence on the Highlands also.   About the
beginning of this period was born John M‘Comie,
the M‘Comie Mor, in whose lifetime the family
rose to its highest point of influence and power in
Perthshire and Forfarshire, and also sank to its
lowest ebb, under powers and circumstances which
the haughty chief was too proud to submit to,
and in his old age unable successfully to resist.
History and tradition alike bear testimony to the
remarkable character of this Highland chief.   The
sagacity and indomitable spirit that characterised
his mental qualities were not more conspicuous
among his contemporaries than his extraordinary
bodily strength.   Sir Æneas M‘Pherson, in his
MS. history, makes mention of " John M‘Intosh
of Forter, commonly called M‘Comie," as among
" the oldest and wisest not only of my own, but
of all our neighbour families ; . . . all men of
sense and reputation, and most of them so very
old that if they were not acquainted with Finla
Mor himself, they were at least personally known
to his children."   John M‘Comie could not have
been acquainted with Finla Mor, but might have

been personally acquainted with his children, his own mother being a granddaughter of Finla Mor.

Sir Æneas M'Pherson speaks of John M'Intosh, or M'Comie, as of Forter, of which barony he had obtained a wadset from the Earl of Airlie, some time between 1651 [1] and 1660. After entering on possession of Forter, he built a mansion-house on the estate at Crandart, where he took up his residence. Crandart is situated on the right bank of the Isla, about a mile and a half north of the old castle of Forter, which had been burned down by Argyll in 1640. Before proceeding further with the history of the M'Comies, it is necessary to describe the main features of the lands held by them in Perthshire and Forfarshire.

Finnegand, that had been so long in the possession of the M'Comies, lies wholly on the right bank of the Shee, in the parish of Kirkmichael, Perthshire. On the south-east corner, opposite Dalnaglar, the land on the side of the Shee at its lowest point is over 1000 feet above sea-level. For

[1] Appendix, Note E.

about two miles along the Shee, which from the
mansion-house of Finnegand turns a little to the
west, there is a belt of arable land, consisting of
level haughs and gently sloping fields, extending
from two to three hundred yards from the water-
side ; then a series of rounded heights, of no great
elevation, leads to the foot of the range of mountains forming the watershed between Glenshee
and the glens with their tributary streams stretching southwards to Strathardle. The land, with
an easterly and north-easterly slope and aspect,
is of moderate fertility; and from its height above
sea-level is better adapted for green than white
crops—grain crops being fully matured only in
very favourable seasons. At about half a mile
from the Shee, the mountains rise rather abruptly,
culminating in Meall Odhar and Meall Uaine,
the latter being 2600 feet above sea-level. On
the opposite side of the Shee from Finnegand
lies Broughdearg, also with its belt of arable land
on the left bank of the Shee, and the mountains
forming the watershed between Glenshee and
Glenisla rising steeply behind it. The highest

point between Broughdearg and Glenisla is Meal-
na-letter, 2297 feet above sea-level, which is on
the boundary-line between Perthshire and Forfarshire, and looks down towards the east upon
Crandart. Farquharson of Broughdearg, it will be
seen, *marched* both west and east with M'Comie
Mor—on the west with Finnegand, on the east
with the barony of Forter, and the large tract of
forest-ground in the extreme north of Glenisla.
The result, with ill-defined boundary-lines, and
unconquerable courage and unyielding pride in
both chieftains, was disastrous to both.

The property of Dalmunzie, held by the descendants of Angus Og, lies about two miles
north-west of Finnegand, immediately west of
the Spittal of Glenshee, and is still held by a
M'Intosh. Glenbeg, in which the M'Comies had
a shealing, lies north of the Spittal of Glenshee,
marching with Braemar on the north.

The barony of Forter, on which the mansion-
house of Crandart was to become the headquarters of the family of M'Combie, is situated in the
west of Forfarshire, in the parish of Glenisla, and

B

extends from Mount Blair, 2441 feet, on the
south, to Cairn - na - Glasha, 3484 feet, on the
north. For about four miles from the eastern
base of Mount Blair northwards, the Isla is the
eastern boundary; it then includes both sides of
the Isla, the boundary being the watershed between Glencally and the Isla, over the summit
of Finalty, 2954 feet. On the north the boundary is formed by the watershed between Canness
glen — Canness burn being the north - eastern
branch of the Isla — and the glen of the Doll,
down which rushes the Whitewater to join the
South Esk, and the watershed between Canlochan glen, the burn of which is the north-western
branch of the Isla, and Glencallater in Aberdeenshire. Between Canness and the head of the
glen of the Doll the highest summit is Tom
Buidhe, 3140 feet; between Canlochan and Glencallater the highest summit is Cairn-na-Glasha.
On the west, the broad-crowned Glas Maol, 3502
feet, near the summit of which the shires of Aberdeen, Perth, and Forfar meet, is the culminating
point of Forfarshire. Thence the boundary-line

goes along the top of Craig Leacach, 3238 feet, which descends in almost a sheer precipice to the Brighty burn, which rises far up the Glas Maol. On the western side of Craig Leacach is Glenbeg, which runs south to the Spittal of Glenshee. At Cairn Aighe, 2824 feet, the boundary-line turns south-eastward to Monamenach, 2649 feet, about two miles north-north-west of Crandart, and thence in a southerly direction to the height overlooking Dalnaglar and the Balloch, whence it sweeps round south-eastwards to Mount Blair again. The length of this district, from Mount Blair to Cairn-na-Glasha, is about ten miles, the breadth varying from one to four miles. The low-lying arable ground extends from the Balloch, 1000 feet, to Auchavan and the Linns, about 1250 feet. Much of this is a friable fertile soil. Above the 1250 feet line, much fine summer pasture-land stretches up the mountain-sides to about 2000 feet. The scenery around Forter is picturesque; above Forter, Glenisla is narrow, the steep mountain-sides closing in on the narrow bottom of the glen. Above the Tulchan, Glenisla contains some of the finest mountain and glen scenery in Scotland. To the left, going up the right bank of the Isla, Monega rises precipitously to the height of 2917 feet, its lower slope for about a mile below the junction of Canlochan and Canness being well wooded. In front, the towering promontory that divides Canlochan from Canness rises grandly and abruptly. The lower part is thickly wooded, then the scarred rocky face, with thin lines of trees struggling up wherever they can find sufficient soil, rises steep and grand to the height of nearly 3000 feet. To the right, Canness, a narrow gorge, wooded on its western side for about a mile from its junction with Canlochan, penetrates for about two miles, first in a north-easterly, then in a north-westerly direction, towards the head-waters of Glencallater. To the left is Canlochan, the glory of Glenisla. From the north-east shoulder of Monega an escarpment runs right round the head of Canlochan, and back to the water-parting between Canlochan and Canness, a distance of over four miles, the top of the escarpment the whole way

being from a little under to a little over 3000
feet above sea-level. Where the waters of Canness and Canlochan meet, the height above
sea-level is 1500 feet; so that there is a precipitous wall of from 1000 feet to 1500 feet running round Canlochan, indented with rugged
and broken rocky gorges. The glen is about
two miles long, running first in a north-westerly
direction, then turning almost due north to Cairn-
na-Glasha. From its south-eastern end, for about
a mile, it is wooded for a considerable distance
up the precipitous face. Beyond this the surface
is bare, with here and there rocky faces rising
sheer and abrupt, in the crevices of which grow
some very rare alpine plants, the exact habitat of
which is known only to a few enthusiastic bot-
anists, who keep their knowledge from ordinary
mortals with jealous care. After passing the
Tulchan, the eye discovers fresh beauties at
every step. The Isla, winding through grassy
haughs, the light rich green of the grass contrast-
ing with the deeper and darker green of the
larch wood, and both with the purple of the

heather; the rocks seamed with red scaurs, jutting at first here and there through the wood, then rising sheer and abrupt over it,—present a picture of beauty and grandeur altogether unrivalled in Forfarshire, and with few equals in the Highlands of Scotland.

Between the Brighty—which, rising far up the Glas Maol, flows first south by the base of Craig Leacach, and then east till it joins the Isla at the Tulchan—and the Isla, below the junction of Canness and Canlochan burns, there lies on the west side of Monega a small ravine or gully called the Glascorrie, the burn from which falls into the Isla, after a south and then south-easterly course, nearly a mile above the junction of the Brighty and Isla. Glen Brighty is black and bare, the only feature in the landscape that attracts the eye being the precipitous face of Craig Leacach, destitute of vegetation and covered with loose shingle. Such is a brief outline of the property of the M'Comie Mor in Glenisla.

Coming now to the personal history of M'Comie Mor, we shall first take up the traditionary tales,

which are still preserved, both in Glenshee and
Glenisla, of his intrepid bravery and immense
personal strength. The first of these refers to the
time he resided at Finnegand.

Those passing along the Highland road from
Blairgowrie to Braemar, may observe a large
stone on the west side of the road, about opposite
to Dalnaglar, and about a mile south from Finnegand. This stone is known by the few Gaelic-
speaking people in the district as Clach-na-
Coileach—the stone of the cock; by those who
speak Scotch, as Cocksteen, which originated as
follows. Proprietors in Glenshee — and most if
not all those in the Blackwater district — in the
fifteenth and sixteenth centuries, held their lands
by feu-charter from the then Earls of Athole, who
levied kain—that is, so many fowls annually, as
a tax or rent—from every reeking house on the
various properties. The term is probably derived
from the Gaelic *ceann*, a head—as this tribute
would consist of so many head of whatever kind
of live stock the kain had to be paid in. This
annual gathering of kain by the Athole men,

while M'Comie Mor was in Finnegand, had gone
on peacefully one year, from the head of the glen
down to a small cot above Finnegand.   Here the
kain-gatherers, finding a poor widowed woman—
a tenant of M'Comie Mor—heartlessly took not
only their lawful kain, but all her stock of poultry,
despite her most urgent entreaties to leave at
least some of them, in pity for her circumstances.
We can easily conceive that the retainers of the
powerful Earl of Athole carried matters with a ·
high hand, as in those times there was practically
no redress of grievances except by the strong
arm.   The widow's only strength lay in tears and
entreaties; and finding these of no avail, she be-
thought her of the strong arm of M'Comie Mor,
if only he could be persuaded to aid her.   There
was no time to lose; for the kain - gatherers
were making their way down the glen, and her
treasured poultry would soon be irretrievably beyond reach.   In all haste she set out for Finnegand, with many tears laid her complaint
before M'Comie Mor, and to her great joy he
at once consented to accompany her to ask re-

dress. We can picture the widow, with heart already lightened—for who would dare to refuse what M'Comie Mor asked in Glenshee?—trudging along by the side of her stalwart protector, and relating all the circumstances of her visitors' harsh words and still harsher deeds. It would not be difficult to find the kain-gatherers, as their progress would be accompanied by the shrill " scraichs" of the captured cocks and hens, mingled, no doubt, with equally shrill objurgations in Gaelic from irate goodwives, whose ideas of what should be taken and what should be left would doubtless differ widely from those of the Athole men. M'Comie Mor and the widow came up with them near the big stone, when the former explained the circumstances of the poor widow, and asked that at least part of her poultry might be returned to her, especially as they had taken more from her than they had a right to. To the widow's great surprise and renewed grief, this reasonable demand was met with a decided refusal, couched in terms the reverse of polite. There was nothing for it, then, but to return to her cot, and put up with her loss as she best could. But if the widow was to be content with silent submission to those with part right, and seemingly whole might, on their side, not so M'Comie Mor. It was bad enough to be refused, but to be spoken to with insolence on his own ground, when making a reasonable request for one of his own dependants, was intolerable. The civil request for the restitution of part of the widow's fowls became a peremptory command to deliver up the whole. The command meeting with no better reception than the request, was at once followed up by M'Comie Mor drawing his sword and attacking the leader of the band. The kain-gatherers at once set down their creels, and rushed to their leader's assistance. But he was *hors de combat* before assistance could reach him; and the astonished Athole men soon found that might as well as right was on the side of the widow, for wherever a blow from M'Comie Mor's right arm fell, there fell an Athole man also. As by this time a good few Glenshee men were arriving, who had learned what was going on, the

Athole men wisely gave way. M'Comie Mor
then advanced and unceremoniously cut open the
coops containing the widow's feathered treasures,
whereupon one crouse young cock mounted the
big stone, and sent forth a shrill, clear, and tri-
umphant pæan of victory. That was a scene not
likely soon to be forgotten in Glenshee : the poor
widow, doubtless but a moment before in an agony
of fear for the safety of her chivalrous champion,
risking his life against such heavy odds on her
behalf, now gladly pouring forth her thanks, while
rejoicing over her recovered treasures : the crest-
fallen kain-gatherers making off with what kain
was still left to them — doubtless strictly civil
and honest in their further requisitions while
in Glenshee; the stalwart chief sheathing his
sword; and high over all the brave little chan-
ticleer, sending forth his notes of defiance to all
the race of Athole kain-gatherers. The scene
was not likely to be forgotten, and is not forgotten; for the Clach-na-Coileach still remains,
a mute but steadfast witness: and often is the
story told in Glenshee of how M'Comie Mor

supplied the much-needed might for the widow's right.

But the quarrel about the kain, as might be expected, did not end here. The Earl of Athole, as superior of the district, could not brook the insult of having his retainers routed, and his kain withheld by a vassal. A well-armed band was, therefore, sent from Athole to Glenshee, to bring M'Comie Mor to Blair Athole dead or alive. In due time they reached Finnegand, and surprised the laird unarmed in the house. But M'Comie Mor had sagacity and wit, as well as strength and courage. The Athole men having explained their errand, he frankly admitted that, in the circumstances, he was powerless to gainsay them. However, it was a pretty long way to Blair Castle, and both they and himself would be better of having some refreshment before setting out. Orders were at once given for refreshments to be set down in the other end of the house; the Athole men and the laird being at this time in the kitchen. While the servants busied themselves in preparing a substantial repast, M'Comie

Mor, by his frank and genial bearing, soon put
the Athole men at their ease. When it was
intimated that their repast was ready, the laird
courteously requested them to lay aside their
arms and plaids, that they might be at more
freedom while eating and drinking. As he himself was unarmed, and all distrust of their enter-
tainer had vanished under the influence of his
unexpected affability, the Athole men piled their
arms in a corner of the kitchen ; and removing
their plaids, followed the host to the other end of
the house, where they found a profuse abundance
of Highland cheer set forth. Charmed by their
host's genial frankness, and softened by unlimited
uisge-beatha, the Athole men were now completely
at their ease, and were doubtless mentally con-
gratulating themselves on the unexpected ease
and pleasure with which they were carrying out
a mission, which they had calculated would be
one of no little danger and difficulty. When,
therefore, their host at length asked permission
to go and give some necessary instructions to his
family about the management of his affairs while

he would be absent, rendered necessary by his being so unexpected called away without notice, the permission was at once granted, without the slightest feeling of mistrust on the part of the Athole men. Accordingly, M'Comie Mor went out, telling them he would send word when he was ready. After waiting a short time, a servant announced that her master was ready. The Athole men at once proceeded to the kitchen to resume their plaids and arms, and found— M'Comie Mor standing fully armed, their plaids all laid out on a table, but not a single gun nor sword to be seen in the corner where they had so imprudently left them. Their lately so genial host then informed them in a haughty tone, that as they had been sent for him, they were at liberty to try and take him with them, but that he was determined to defend his liberty to the utmost of his power. The dismay of the Athole men may be imagined. Even had they been again armed, they knew full well by this time how extremely dangerous a task it would have been to have overpowered him; as it was, it

would have been but throwing their lives away
to have attempted his capture. There was
nothing for it then but to resume their plaids,
and return unarmed to Athole, and explain, as
they best might, the ignominious failure of their
mission.

As a matter of course, M'Comie Mor did not
expect that the Earl of Athole would quietly
submit to this fresh indignity. An unforeseen
event, however, brought the matter to a more
friendly termination than could otherwise have
been looked for. Shortly after the unsuccessful
attempt to carry off M'Comie Mor to Athole, a
professional champion swordsman, or bully as he
was called, a gigantic Italian, made his appearance at Blair Athole, and as usual challenged the
best man the Earl of Athole could produce to
fight; and in the event of no one accepting his
challenge, or any one accepting it and being
beaten, he would claim, as a right, a sum of
money, as a sort of tribute earned by his
prowess. The payment of the money was a
less source of annoyance to one in the position

of the Earl of Athole than the thought that in
all the wide district of which he was superior,
he could not find a man of sufficient strength
and courage to successfully cope with this foreign
bravo.   And in proportion also to the disgrace
of having no man in Athole a match for him,
would be the glory to the Earl and his vassals
if he could produce an Athole champion able to
conquer such a redoubted hero.   In the present
instance, disgrace instead of honour appeared
likely to fall on Athole and Athole men; for a
sight of the foreigner, who was of immense
size and fierce aspect, together with the no-
toriety of his extraordinary skill as a swordsman, proved sufficient to deter the strongest and
bravest of the Athole men from risking life and
limb in a fight with him.   In this emergency, the
Earl at last reflected that M'Comie Mor, who
had recently lowered the prestige of the Athole
men as their opponent, was the very man to
raise it again as their champion.   We can easily
understand that at a time when personal prowess
was of such account, the Earl's displeasure at

the double indignity offered to his immediate retainers was tempered with a feeling of satisfaction that he had amongst his vassals a man possessed of such unusual strength, courage, and sagacity. It was evident, also, to a prudent man, that it would be a more satisfactory termination to the present quarrel that M'Comie Mor should give satisfaction to the Earl's offended dignity by rendering a personal service to him, than that so brave a man should be subdued by mere force of numbers. Accordingly, a trusted retainer was despatched to Finnegand, who was to explain to M'Comie Mor that if he would come to Blair Castle, and there render a personal service to the Earl of an honourable nature, that in that case the Earl would look on this as making full amends for the indignities inflicted on his retainers on their last two visits. For some time M'Comie Mor was in great doubt as to this intimation being made in good faith, and had a strong suspicion that it was merely a ruse to get him quietly into Athole, where satisfaction would be required of him for the affair of the kain-gatherers, and his outwitting the second expedition. Assured at length that the Earl's invitation was made in good faith, he set out with the messenger, and arrived at Blair Castle. But here a fresh difficulty arose. On being confronted with the Italian champion, and the purpose for which he had been summoned explained to him, he flatly refused to fight with any man with whom he had no quarrel. At this unlooked-for declaration, the hopes of the Athole men, which had been raised to a great height, from the account given by the kain-gatherers of his extraordinary strength and courage, and from his magnificent personal appearance, received a rude fall. In vain the Earl urged and entreated him, in vain some of the Athole men began audibly to hint that the redoubted M'Comie Mor's courage had vanished like their own at the sight of the fierce and stalwart Italian. This latter worthy's behaviour soon brought about the desired result. On learning that the man who was expected to fight with him refused to do so on the plea that there was no quarrel between them, and therefore no occasion to fight, he at once attributed this to cowardice, and began to indulge in much high-sounding bravado. This having no effect, he next proceeded to personal indignity, and approaching his apparently imperturbable opponent, he with one hand lifted his kilt, and with the other—*horresco referens*—bestowed a sounding whack on the astounded chief's posteriors. In an instant, with the peculiarly graceful sweep that always marked the drawing of his sword— a peculiarity which afterwards stood him in good stead on another occasion—his sword was out of its scabbard. The Italian immediately sprang back, and put himself in position. The Athole men now silent, in breathless suspense watched the two gigantic opponents, for there was that on the face of M'Comie Mor that showed it was to be a battle *à outrance.* Nor were the spectators held long in suspense as to the result. A few careful parries, and almost before they could comprehend or believe what they saw, M'Comie Mor's blade, with lightning-like rapidity and extraordinary force, was through the Italian's guard,

and his fighting career in this world was for ever
ended.

Another incident of his life while at Finnegand
marks both the proud spirit of M'Comie Mor and
his determination not to put up with any slight to
himself or family, and also shows the lawlessness[1]
of the time, and the little regard for human life.
One day on coming home to Finnegand, he found
his wife and the female servants in a very excited
state, and on inquiry found that a big strong *caird*
had called, and finding no man about the place,
had behaved very rudely to his wife.   Ascertain-
ing that the caird had gone up the glen, he took
two swords with him, and immediately followed
in pursuit.   Coming up with him opposite Broughdearg, he gave him his choice of the swords, and
the result of the fight that followed between them
was the slaughter of the caird, who was buried
where he fell, and the place is still known as
Imir-a-Chaird, the Caird's ridge or field.[2]

After obtaining the wadset of the barony of
Forter, and building the mansion-house at Cran-

---

[1] Appendix, Note F.   [2] Appendix, Note G.

dart, M'Comie Mor left Finnegand and resided at Crandart, the house of which was built in 1660. By the time he came to reside there he was past his prime, and had become less desirous of exerting his personal strength, it is therefore probable that his famous feat with the stone, which since then has been known as M'Comie Mor's putting-stone, was performed while he was yet a young man at Finnegand. The place where the feat was performed, and the stone itself, and the stance, are all remarkable. The source of the Prosen, a right-bank tributary of the South Esk, is at the west end of the slope that reaches back from the summit of the Mayar, 3043 feet, whose eastern side rises abruptly over Glen Prosen. At the west end of this slope, in two slight depressions which spread out like a V, are gathered the head-waters of the Prosen, a short distance from the source of the Cally, a left-bank tributary of the Isla. Between the two depressions is a comparatively level meadow of short benty grass, and from the surface of this meadow the upper edge of an earthfast stone, about 4 or 5 feet long, projects for about 6 inches above the surface. This projecting edge of the boulder forms the stance, and about 26 feet beyond this stance is embedded, in a round hole in the ground, a round-shaped rough-surfaced stone of about 35 lb. in weight, and local tradition for over two hundred years has handed down the hole, in which the stone lies embedded to about half its diameter, as the mark to which M'Comie Mor putted the stone from the stone stance. On many of the surrounding heights, pieces of ground as smooth and level may be got; but so good a natural stance and natural putting-stone is extremely rare, if not altogether unique, on a mountain-top. It is easy to understand that all the conditions and materials being found so handy, for such a national pastime as putting the stone, by the young men of the surrounding glens, when on hunting expeditions or looking after their flocks, the place would soon become well known; the marks of noted throwers would be pointed out, and every noted putter would be anxious to put a best on record down if possible. There is nothing improbable, therefore, in believing that the mark put in over two hundred years ago by admiring contemporaries, and kept fresh by succeeding generations, points out the exact spot to which M'Comie Mor putted the present stone from the present stance. Many athletes of the present day have made a pilgrimage to it when passing between Clova and Glenisla, and to both them and their forefathers stance, stone, and mark have ever remained the same. What renders it still more probable is, that the same stone could be putted the same distance by one or two of the leading athletes of the present time. Most traditionary putting-stones of bygone heroes are of a weight, or have been putted a distance, that at once stamps the accounts given as absurd nonsense.

On the west side of the westmost arm of the V, the strongest spring that there gushes out is known as M'Comie Mor's well. From the top of the Mayar, looking north, the top of Benachie, beyond the vale of Alford, may be seen through a gap, as it were, among the intervening mountains. Perhaps it was a glimpse of distant Ben-

achie from this point that led young Donald
M'Combie in after-years, when the fortunes of
his family were on the wane in Forfarshire, to
seek his fortune in the Vale of Alford. Besides
that of the well-known putting-stone, other traditions exist of M'Comie Mor's great personal
strength. Two stones used to be pointed out
in Canlochan, with which he performed feats
altogether beyond the power of ordinary men.
He is also said to have become possessed of a
bull in the Stormont district, which had become
unmanageable from its fierce temper, on very
easy terms from his point of view. M'Comie
Mor hearing the owner of the bull saying he
would have to destroy him, as he was become
unmanageable and unsafe, laughed at the idea of
a man being beat by a bull. The owner, said to
have been Mercer of Meikleour, nettled at being
laughed at, said that if M'Comie Mor could
manage the bull unaided, he would get him home
with him as a present. This offer being accepted,
they proceeded to the enclosure where the fierce
brute was confined, which no sooner saw them

than he rushed bellowing to the side of the fence.
M'Comie Mor, reaching over the fence, with his
left hand seized the bull's right horn, then vault-
ing over the fence, seized his other horn with his
right hand, and in a moment had the now in-
furiated brute on his back. Then allowing him
to regain his feet, he immediately overthrew him
a second time, and this he repeated till he was
thoroughly subdued, when he was afterwards
taken home in triumph by his conqueror.[1]

In an age when witches were still believed in
by ministers of the Gospel, and duly punished or
exorcised, and the black art had its schools of
learning, it is quite natural that several traditionary incidents in M'Comie Mor's life should contain supernatural elements. There is still pointed
out a large stone forming the lintel of the lime-
kiln at Crandart, which, after baffling the efforts
of the old chief and his sons, was placed there
by one man. The story goes that this man,
Knox Baxter, *alias* Colin M'Kenzie, by name,
who was suspected of being possessed of black

---

[1] Appendix, Note H.

art, came to Crandart as M'Comie and his sons
were trying ineffectually to get the stone into its
place. Sitting down a little apart, he viewed un-
concernedly the efforts put forth, without volun-
teering a helping hand. By-and-by the dinner-
hour came, without the stone having been got
into position. Having excused himself from
accepting the invitation given him to dinner,
the stranger was left sitting by the kiln-side,
where he was found when they returned to continue their work at the kiln, but the stone was
now in the place where the united efforts of
M'Comie Mor and his sons had failed to place
it ! It is said the old chief made no comment
on this startling feat, but quietly divesting
himself of his coat with its silver buttons, he
handed it to Knox Baxter as a tacit acknow-
ledgment of the estimation he had of his powers.
The old chief knew that no man unaided could
have done what had been done, and deemed it
prudent to propitiate his uncanny visitor.

But a still more exciting and uncanny adventure
awaited him. In going through the forest of Can-

lochan one day he came upon no less a being
than the water-kelpie's wife, in the weird and
secluded Glascorrie. Taken unawares, this redoubted fairy or elf had not time to escape to
the water before M'Comie Mor had her firmly
in his grasp. But how to get her to Crandart?
He knew that if he crossed running water with
her she would escape from him, do what he
might. He therefore set out on a long and difficult route homewards, around the head-waters of
the Brighty, along the summits of Craig Leacach,
Cairn Aighe, Black Hill, and Monamenach, then
cautiously threading the mountain-side above
Crandart, and nearly losing his precious capture
while incautiously stepping over an almost in-
visible streamlet, he at length landed her safely
at Crandart. Arrived there, his unwilling visitor
had to bargain for her release, the condition being
that the chief should have some circumstance relating to the time, place, or manner of his death
foretold him. Thereupon the fairy, taking him
to the face of the hill above Crandart, pointed
out a large stone, and told him he would die

with his head above it. Having now acquired her liberty, she departed to her own haunts again, and we may be sure was careful never to be so incautious in her future wanderings in Canlochan. M'Comie Mor took prudent precautions that dying with his head above the stone pointed out by the fairy should prove more convenient than its then position warranted. He therefore caused the stone to be removed from the hillside, and built into the wall of his house at Crandart, so that the head of the stone was under the head of his bed, whereon many years after he died, with his head above the stone, as the fairy foretold.

As John M'Comie advanced in life and found his personal strength diminishing, he was anxious that his eldest son and successor might be worthy of the family name, but seems to have had some doubts on this point, as although the young man, who was also named John, had obtained the cognomen of Mor, big, from his stalwart appearance, yet his quiet peaceable disposition had led the old chief to imagine he was too gentle—had, as

he said, too much of the Campbell blood in him.
This, according to M'Comie Mor's opinion, was
not likely to increase his courage; he therefore
determined to put it to the test, and thereby set
his mind at rest. Knowing that his son would
be returning from Glenshee to Glenisla one even-
ing about dusk by the pass of Glen Bainie, he
there lay in wait for him at a sort of natural
stone seat, still called M'Comie Mor's Chair.
Having disguised himself as much as possible,
he trusted to the deepening twilight sufficiently
concealing his identity. No sooner, then, did his
son appear, than, without uttering a word of challenge or warning, he at once sprang up, drew his
sword, and attacked him. It has been already
mentioned that M'Comie Mor was distinguished
by the peculiarly graceful sweep with which he
drew his sword when about to fight. His son
fortunately observed this, and at once suspected
both who his adversary was and the reason for
this unexpected attack. Keeping his suspicions
to himself, however, he at once began to defend
himself, while demanding the reason of the attack.

His demand meeting with no attention from his silent aggressor, he gave all his attention to the matter on hand, and exerting his utmost skill, strength, and agility, he began to press his opponent in the most determined manner, and at length disarmed him, and had him completely at his mercy. He then told his exhausted and —for the first time in his life—defeated assailant, that if he wished to save his life he must at once reveal his name, and give his reason for so unprovoked an attack. At the first sound of his father's voice, his son immediately began to reproach him for thus endangering both their lives, and told him that he could have slain him more than once during the combat, and probably would have done so, had he not suspected from his manner of drawing his sword and beginning the attack who he was, and reminded him of how awful a thing it would have been for the survivor had either of them slain the other; to all of which the old chief, highly elated by his son's unquestionable courage, strength, and skill, contentedly replied that all that was of no consequence compared with the now, to his mind, clearly demonstrated fact that his son was a true M'Comie.

Leaving tradition, we now come to the historical part of the history of John M'Comie, and it will be found that it is far more exciting and tragical than anything handed down by tradition. To understand how the strange and stirring events towards the close of John M'Comie's life originated, we must bear in mind that he had entered into possession of the barony of Forter during the time of the Commonwealth. In these unsettled and unsettling times, such a man as John M'Comie could not remain inactive. At the outset he had sided with the King's party,[1] and in Chambers's 'History of the Rebellion in Scotland' we find, in vol. ii., appendix, under date February 11, 1645, as forfaulted for "the invasione of the Northe,"[2] John M'Colmie.[3] There is no doubt, however, but that he changed sides, and it is probable this was in great measure owing to his being married to

[1] Appendix, Note A.   [2] Appendix, Note I.   [3] Appendix, Note J.

Elizabeth Campbell, granddaughter of Donald Campbell of Denhead, near Coupar-Angus, who was a son of Donald Campbell, last Abbot of Coupar in Angus, and fourth son of Archibald, Earl of Argyll. It was doubtless this connection by marriage with a scion of the House of Argyll that induced John M'Comie to side with the Parliament and Cromwell latterly. This change of sides proved most disastrous to him and his family, for no sooner was the Restoration an accomplished fact, than the Royalists, who had before feared and respected him, began to harass him in person and property. Charles II. was restored in May 1660, entering London on the 29th of May, and in less than a year afterwards the Scottish Parliament passed an "Act and Decreit in favour of James, Earle of Airlie, against Johne M'Intosh, *alias* M'Comie, of Forthar," at Edinburgh, May 3, 1661. From which Act it appears that the Earl's father, James, Lord Ogilvie, had raised letters of free forestry for the forest of Glascorrie, commonly called Camlochan, in the reign of James VI., as had also the then Earl in the reign of Charles I. Yet, notwithstanding, " The said Johne M'Intosh, *alias* M'Comie, upon ane secreit design to incroach upon the supplicant's glen of Glascoric, comonly called Camlochan, did eat the grass of the said forrest, cut down and destroy the growing trees, and kill the roes and dears haunting and feiding therein at his pleasure." John M'Comie had obtained a sight of these letters and " gave ane inventar subscryved with his hand for redeliverie thereof, . . . but flatlie refused so to doe." So cannot get them, though " neidfull to the supplicant and James, Lord Ogilvie, his sonne." " And the said John M'Comie, defender, compeiring personally with Mr George M'Kenzie[1] his pro^r, . . . and alledged that he ought not to redeliver the same Because be verteu of ane contract of alienation betuixt the persewer and defender The persewer is obleidged to deliver to him the said writs *et quod frustra petit qui mox est restiturus.* Whereunto it was replyed for the said persewer that he opposed the band and in-

[1] Appendix, Note K.

D

ventar subscryved with his hand for redelyverie
of the same, To the which it wes duplyed for the
said defender, that the yeers wherein the persewer had libertie to redeim the said glen of
Glascorie from the defender not being expyred
the time of the granting of the saids inventars,
as they are now, he could not be tyed be verteu
therof to deliver the same, his right to the said
glen being now irredeimable, and the writs his
oune.   All which being set forth, His Maiestie,
with advice and consent of the saids estates of
Parliament," ordained that the letters of free
forestry be given up.

From which it would appear that the defence
of John M'Comie lay, first, in the fact that the
deed of alienation gave him the right to the
letters, and that it was needless to give back to
Lord Airlie what he would immediately have to
redeliver again ; second, that the time which had
been given to the Earl of Airlie to redeem the
forest had expired, and that as the engagement
to redeliver the letters referred only to the time
during which the forest could be redeemed, the

letters of free forestry were, like the forest itself,
beyond recall, and were now the property of
John M'Comie, not of Lord Airlie. In the Act
there is no attempt to deny John M'Comie's
statements. Judgment was simply given against
him, the reason for which appears in certain
phrases in an "Act and Remit, James, Earle of
Airlie, against Johne M'Intoshe, *alias* M'Comie, of
Forther." "Anent the supplication given in to
the Estates of Parliament be James, Earle of
Airlie, and James, Lord Ogilvie, his sonne, against
Johne M'Intosh, *alias* M'Comie, of Forther, shew-
ing That be ane contract of alienation passed
betuixt the supplicant and the said Johne M'Intosh, anent the alienation to him of the lands and
baronie of Forther, Ther is expreslie reserved
to the supplicant the forest and glen of Glascorie,
comonly called Camlochan, lyand within the
parochen of Glenyla and Shereffdome of Forfar,
and bounded within the particular meiths and
marches mentioned in the said contract : Notwithstanding of the which reservation, the said
John M'Intosh, *alias* M'Comie, *haveing great*

power with the late vsurpers as their intelligencer and favourite, had these severall yeers bygone encroached within the meiths and marches of the said forrest, and had pastured yeerly thereon above fyvescore oxen and twenty milk kyne with diverse horses. For remeid whairof the supplicant intendit action of cognition of marches and molestation against the said John M'Comie befor the Shirreff of Forfar, founded vpon the Act of Parliament, In which action ther being diverse disputes, ansuers, duplys, and triplyes made for either partie and set doun in writ, The same wes at lenth delivered to Mr David Nevay, Shirreff of Forfar, to be advised be him, who being readie to pronounce interloquitur therein, The said Johne M'Comie, *be his said moyen and favour with the English vsurpers*, purchased ane advocation of the said persute, and produced the same befor the said Shirreff depute, thereby to stop and discharge him from any further proceiding therein, Albeit upon most false and unjust grounds. . . . Since the production of the which advocation not only the forsaid action and per-

sute had sisted and sleeped, Bot also the said
Johne M'Comie had continewed yeerly sensyne
pasturing his goods and cattell vpon the said
forrest, and eiting and destroying the haill grasse
thairof, to the supplicants' great hurt, preiudice,
and heavie oppression. . . . Thereupon His
Majestie, with advice and consent of the saids
estates of Parliament, having considered the said
supplication, . . . and the said defender nor his
said pro⸱ had proposed no reasonable cause why
the desire of the said petition ought not to be
granted,"— thereupon remits to Sheriff to settle
marches. Here we have the reason of the
summary settlement of the matters in dispute.
It is admitted that John M'Comie had had full
and complete possession of the forest of Canlochan for years past, and that he had got
discharge "from any further proceeding" anent
his right. But he had got all this, it was alleged,
because of his "moyen and favour with the
English usurpers," and on account of his "having great power with the late usurpers as their
intelligencer and favourite." For such a one

against a Royalist nobleman there was little hope of a favourable issue in any court of law of that period, and in Parliament none whatever. That Lord Airlie placed his hopes of success not on a decision according to law, but on the political feeling of the time, is shown by his bringing the matter in dispute, not before the ordinary legal tribunals, but before Parliament. To the Restoration Parliament the matter would appear very simple. Here is Lord Airlie, one of ourselves, who, while our party was held in subjection by the late usurpers, alienated a valuable part of his property to one in power and favour with these usurpers. This deed of alienation has become irredeemable, but Lord Airlie says this was owing to the position of the respective parties at the time, the usurpers having great power, the Royalists little or no power. Lord Airlie, therefore, wants his property back again, which we, as the party now in power, will now give him, putting aside all question of the legality or justice of our decision.[1]

[1] Appendix, Note L.

As showing still further to what extent John M'Comie was a marked man, and disliked by the Government of the Restoration, we learn from the Acts of Parliament of Scotland, vol. vii. p. 426, that he was amongst the "exceptions from the Act of Indemnity, Sept. 9, 1662, in so far as may concern the payment of the sumes under-written," — viz., "Johne Malcolmè of Forthar, 1800 pds."

In 1665 John Mackintosh of Forter in Glenisla, with twenty-five Farquharsons under William of Inverey, and George Farquharson of Brough-dearg in Glenshee, were among 500 men who attended the summons of the chief of the M'Intoshes, to meet at the Kirk of Insh. It is also worthy of note that Forbes of Skellater joined the M'Intoshes at the same muster.

Broughdearg, opposite to Finnegand in Glen-shee, and marching with the barony of Forter in Glenisla, was held in the time of John M'Comie by Farquharsons. The proprietor about the time of the Restoration was Robert Farquharson, who had sought the hand of John M'Comie's daughter in marriage, and had been accepted, but had afterwards changed his mind, and married Helen Ogilvie, daughter of Colonel Ogilvie of Shannalie. This slight no doubt rankled in the minds of the M'Comies, and had much to do with the bitterness that subsequently existed between the two families.

Some time after the decisions in his favour, the Earl of Airlie let the grazings of the forest of Canlochan to Farquharson of Broughdearg. But John M'Comie was far from acquiescing in or even obeying an Act of Parliament, when he thought it unjust towards himself. Although Farquharson of Broughdearg had got a tack of the grazings, he by no means got possession, as John M'Comie continued to send his stock to the forest as formerly. Farquharson of course resented this, and the bad feeling between the two families increased, till it found vent in a series of events, so strange, lawless, and exciting, that one can scarcely believe they could have taken place little more than two hundred years ago in Glenisla and Glenshee, where to-day a serious

breach of law or order is rarely or ever heard of.
But we are now on firm historical ground, as the
events we are about to narrate are all duly
chronicled in the Justiciary Records, or Books of
Adjurnal, vol. xiii., 1673. From this we learn
that, on the 1st of January 1669, Robert Farquharson of Broughdearg, and his brothers John
and Alexander, with fifty or sixty others, went
"under cloud and silence of night" to Crandart,
with "swords, durks, pistolls, hagbutts, targes,
halberts, axes, and other weapons," and having
laid themselves in ambush, awaited till near break
of day, when John M'Comie having "had occasion to come abroad about his lawfull affaires,"
they without giving him time even to put on his
clothes, carried him off to Broughdearg. A
strange scene truly, and one little creditable to
the Farquharsons. To surprise an old man, not
only unarmed, but only partially dressed, in the
dark at his own door, was a poor feat for fifty to
sixty men, bristling with arms and armour of all
kinds. It is also to be observed that the Farquharsons were the first to use personal violence

in the quarrel. The force employed, and the mode of capture, both show very forcibly the opinion the Farquharsons entertained of M'Comie Mor's prowess even in his old age. But though the old chief had been thus entrapped, his sons were to be reckoned with. Accordingly, John M'Comie was kept all that day at Broughdearg, but at night was removed to Tombey, which is called in the indictment, "ane wilderness and desert place." It is about a mile or little more westward from Broughdearg, and has still a good deal of natural birch wood upon it, the name meaning the birch thicket or knoll. Here on the following day, John, Alexander, James, Robert, and Mr Angus (Angus it will be observed had been at a university and obtained his degree), came to enter into negotiations for their father's release, when they also were detained as prisoners, until the whole were compelled to give a bond for 1700 merks for their liberty.[1] In the Farquharsons' indictment against the M'Comies, this visit of the sons for the release of their father

[1] Appendix, Note M.

is set down as a raid organised by Mr Angus for
the murder of Broughdearg. Mr Angus is said
to have collected twenty to thirty persons, all
armed with "swords, durks, pistolls, and other
weapons," and knowing that Robert Farquharson was at Tombey, they laid an ambush in a
thicket of wood, near the house of Tombey, and
on the highway, waiting for several hours till he
should come out, on purpose to kill him, and that
they detained several persons that passed by, lest
they should have given Robert Farquharson
intelligence of the ambush. No mention is
made that Mr Angus's father was also at Tombey, in the power of the Farquharsons. To have
slain Robert Farquharson outside the house of
Tombey, while their father was inside it a
prisoner in the power of the Farquharsons,
would have been to have ensured his father's
death, instead of procuring his life and freedom.
And that that was their purpose is clearly proved
by the fact that his release in safety was pro-
cured. It is also difficult to see how, if the
M'Comies had gone with a force of twenty to

thirty men, they could have been kept prisoners, apparently without any trouble. We can, however, believe it quite probable that Mr Angus and his brothers approached Tombey with caution, and also believe that if chance had thrown Robert Farquharson in their way, they would have seized him and kept him in their power, as a guarantee for the release of their father without ransom. But for the reason already given, it is manifest they would not, at that time, have made any attempt on Robert Farquharson's life.   .

So far the Farquharsons had been the aggressors, and might be supposed to be satisfied with their success, and the ransom for which they held the M'Comies' bond. Yet, on the 14th May of the same year, the Farquharsons and their retainers, to the number of thirty-eight, all armed with dirks, pistols, and other weapons, went to the lands of Kilulock, then occupied by Robert M'Comie, son of John M'Comie, and sowed and harrowed the land, although it had already been sowed and harrowed by Robert

M'Comie. At first sight it is difficult to see on what grounds the Farquharsons so repeatedly, and seemingly so wantonly, attacked the M'Comies in person and property. To understand this, it is necessary once more to consider the political situation. During the latter years of the Commonwealth the M'Comies had rapidly increased in power and influence. John M'Comie's marriage with a Campbell had still further increased his ascendancy. But in 1661, the very year that John M'Comie began to be harassed by his enemies, the Marquis of Argyll was executed. With the Restoration, John M'Comie's Royalist neighbours, and chief among them the Ogilvies, at once began to turn the changed fortunes of parties to their own account. As John M'Comie's marriage with a Campbell was at one time a stepping-stone to power, and latterly a weight to drag him down, so Robert Farquharson's marriage to an Ogilvie, which would have been a drawback to his fortunes in the time of the Commonwealth, was now a powerful agency for his advancement. Although the cause of the

breaking off of the marriage between Robert
Farquharson and Miss M'Comie is not mentioned, it is highly probable that the marriage
had been arranged about the time of the fall of
the Commonwealth, and that Farquharson had
drawn back when he saw the turn affairs were
likely to take, and had chosen an alliance with
an Ogilvie and Royalist, as likely to be far more
to his advantage. We have, then, on the one
hand John M'Comie proscribed by the Government of the Restoration for the part he had taken
latterly on the side of the Commonwealth ; already deprived in law of part of what he considered his own property, by the head of the
Ogilvies ; and now attacked in person and property by Farquharson of Broughdearg, who was
to enjoy what he had been deprived of. On the
other hand, Farquharson, allied by marriage with
the Ogilvies, and already, as it were, rewarded
for the slight he had given the M'Comies, by
receiving a tack of the disputed forest of Canlochan, would naturally think that the M'Comies
were now become fair spoil for all who had the

courage to attack them, and that they would be
little likely to resort to law after their recent
experience. In these times of civil war, those
on the losing side were practically at the mercy
of those on the winning side. On the most
frivolous pretexts their right to property would
be disputed, or forcibly taken from them, and an
appeal to law was almost certain to go against
them. Their only hope lay in their own ability
to defend themselves and their possessions. And
the Farquharsons were soon to see that M'Comie
Mor was no longer to be trifled with. Old and
failed though he was in person, and knowing that
there was no one now with power to help him,
his spirit was still undaunted, and he determined
to withstand his enemies with his own strength in
future, and to make retaliation when he saw an
opportunity. Accordingly, we find that the next
incident in the feud was that Robert Farquharson
narrowly escaped with his life in July or August
1670, from the pursuit of James and Alexander,
sons of John M'Comie, and Donald Gerters, John
Burns, and David Guthrie, servants to John

M'Comie, within the forest of Glascorrie ; and
these not appearing to answer for the crime at
the trial in 1673, were " denunced our Sove-
raigne Lord's rebells, and ordained them to be
putt to the horn, and all ther movable goods and
gear to be escheat and imbrought to his Majestie's
use, as fugitives frae the lawes for the crymes
above mentioned — which wes pronunced for
doome." It was on the occasion of Robert
Farquharson's meeting some of John M'Comie's
servants in Glengarmie, which lies to the north-
west of Broughdearg, and south of Glen Brighty,
that on their telling their master "they had let
the defunct gae without any prejudice," John
M'Comie " did either curse, upbraid, or reprove
them for not taking from him ane legg, ane arme,
or his lyff, declairing that if they had done it he
should have bein their warrand." This fact,
brought out at the trial, shows that M'Comie Mor
was now thoroughly roused ; and it is significant,
too, of the effect this had on the Farquharsons,
that we hear no more of the Farquharsons making
personal attacks on the M'Comies. They had

evidently thought that, being now old, and having no one to depend on for help but his own family and dependants, he could be attacked with impunity. Finding now their mistake, they would doubtless have been glad to have let the quarrel drop; and had the M'Comies given up their claim to free forestry in Canlochan, there might have been no further trouble. But the fact of Robert Farquharson's being driven out of the forest showed that his tenure of it was still very precarious. Fearing, however, any longer to attack the M'Comies personally, the Farquharsons seized some of the M'Comies' cattle in 1672, whereupon John M'Comie " persewed a spulzie " against Robert Farquharson before the Sheriff of Forfar, and got letters of caption against him. It is worthy of remark here that John M'Comie sought redress in a legal way. But a new difficulty arose, as Robert Farquharson swore " no man should take him alive," an oath he made good. Accordingly, when Alexander Strachan, the messenger of the burgh of Forfar, went to take Broughdearg, he had to return baffled. So

E

matters stood when, on the 28th January 1673, Robert Farquharson went to Forfar "for his own defence of the said persuit." John M'Comie was aware of Robert Farquharson's going to Forfar on this day, and is said in the indictment to have spoken to his sons "thir words, or to the lyk purpose : Goe to Forfar; arme yourselves with your pistolls and swords; take my servant with you, and bring him dead or alyve. That severall tymes befor that he said he should have his lyff for the many affronts and injuries he had done him, tho' he should ware two of his best sones in the querrell; *and who would or durst speir after it ?*" According to the account given by the Farquharsons, when they reached Forfar, Robert Farquharson was informed that "the Court wes done; whereupon, having no other bussieness at Forfar, he returned, and wes in his journey homewards," when he was attacked by the M'Comies. John, Alexander, James, and Robert, sons of John M'Comie, and J. Burn, T. Fleming, D. Guthrie, and D. M'Intosh, their servants, had gone to Forfar to watch the result of the action before the Sheriff. It is probable, therefore, that the Farquharsons had returned homewards before reaching Forfar, when they heard of the M'Comies being present in some strength. Be this as it may, when the M'Comies heard that the Farquharsons were on their way home again without having put in an appearance before the Sheriff, they got Alexander Strachan, the burgh messenger, so that they might act legally, and went in pursuit of the Farquharsons. By the time they had got the messenger, they were in some uncertainty as to where the Farquharsons were. It is said in the Farquharsons' indictment, that at the house of Torbeg, "they with ther durks and swords stobbed the beds and other places where they imagined him (Robert Farquharson) to have been lurking. . . . Alse did swear every persone they did meit, if they had seen Robert Farquharson." At length they met a poor man, whom they threatened to kill if he would not tell : said man, "in fear of his lyff," told them the Farquharsons were on their way to Loggie. Being informed of which, "the said

Alexander and James M'Comies, and the other remnant persones above named, threw away ther plaids and betook themselves to ther armes, and in a hostill and militarie pouster, persewed and followed after the saids Robert and John Farquharsons, and the said Alexander ther brother, to the lands of Drumgley, where having overtaken the said Robert, they most cruellie and inhumanlie invadit and assaulted the saids Robert and John Farquharsons, and the said Alexander ther brother, and gave them severall shotts and wounds in ther bodies, heads, and hands, off the which the said Robert Farquharson dyed immediatlie upon the place, and the said John Farquharson wes woundit, and therefter dyed of these wounds within days." This is the account of the Farquharsons, which, be it observed, gives no details of the fight, the reason for which we can understand in the light of the details given by the evidence brought forward by the M'Comies. The evidence of the messenger, that should have been impartial and trustworthy, is unfortunately contradictory and unreliable. There was first produced "an execution of caption," which he wrote at "the desyre of the M'Comies—but received neither good deid nor promise of good deid at that time for giving thereof." The execution of caption was to the effect that Robert Farquharson, "being chairged in his Majestie's name to render him prisoner to me—most contemptuouslie disobeyed, and made resistance by drawing of ane sword against me and my assistants, whereupon I brack my wand of peace." This is in accordance with the M'Comies' defence—viz., that the messenger called on them as assistants, and that they were acting legally in trying to capture Robert Farquharson. The letter next produced was written to James Farquharson of Laidnathie, because David Fenton, in Loggie, a friend of the Farquharsons, told him the Farquharsons were all at Kilimuir, and were to take messenger's life unless he would write some such letter. The letter states, that "I wes not within sex pair of butts when he (Robert Farquharson) was killed, and likewise I do declair I never spoke with him that day." Lastly, we have

what professes to be the messenger's impartial
account of the matter as follows : " As to the
matter of fact, declares that he did not speak
with Brughderg that day, nor wes near him be
the space of sex or seven pair of butts when he wes
killed, *but cryed to him about that distance to render
himself prisoner*, and the M'Comies also cryed,
who were running after Brughderg ; does not
know whether he heard either of them, *but cryed
he would be taken be none of them*, and ran through
a mosse and the M'Comies after him." In the
indictment by the M'Comies against the Farquharsons, the account is so circumstantial and
graphic, as to carry conviction of its truth along
with it. It is certain that the messenger, armed
with a legal warrant, cried to Robert Farquharson
to surrender ; it is also certain that Robert Farquharson heard this, as he replied that " he would
be taken be none of them." After this, John
M'Comie, believing that he was acting legally,
overtook Robert Farquharson, and, be it observed,
did not attempt to slay or even injure him, but
merely " so secured him as that he wes not able

to doe any present hurt." And here he gives proof of the mildness of disposition which led his father to doubt his courage. He wanted to make sure that Robert Farquharson should no longer escape answering for the seizure of his father's cattle; but he also wanted this to be effected, if possible, without undue violence, and without bloodshed. While holding Robert Farquharson, he was of course incapable of defending himself from any other one who chose to attack him, and it was while in this position that John and Alexander, brothers to Robert Farquharson, "presented ther guns, and came so near them that *the mouths of ther guns toutched the said John his flank, and fyred upon him, and so disinabled him that he fell to the ground, and by the same shotts killed Robert M'Intosh, the compleaner's other son, dead to the ground;* and ther being nothing to satiat ther inveterat hatred and malice but the said John M'Intosh lyff and his sons, the said John Farquharson in Cantsmilne, —— Farquharson his son, Thomas Creighton in Milntown of Glenisla, *came in cold blood* near to the Mosse of Forfar, wher the said John M'Intosh *wes yet alyve lying in his wounds, and ther with ther durks and swords stobbed and woundit the said John M'Intosh untill he dyed."* More cowardly and dastardly butchery—for it was not fighting— was never perpetrated. From first to last there is no account of any Farquharson attacking a M'Comie in an honourable and straightforward manner ; and now, after shooting John and Robert M'Comie almost in cold blood, they made no further stand, as it was offered to be proved, on their behalf, that the wounds of which Robert Farquharson died on the spot, and John Farquharson his brother died a few days after, *were received in the back.*

The bodies of the slain men were, it is said, brought home by different routes, by the advice of prudent counsellors, lest there might be a fresh outbreak between the two families and their servants and adherents, if they should meet together in the then excited state of their feelings. The M'Comies were buried in the churchyard of Glenisla.

We can form some idea of the feelings of grief and exasperation that filled the heart of John M'Comie, from the following expressions, cited during the trial as being used by him after the intelligence of what he termed the murder of his sons, reached Crandart. It is stated that "severall tymes, when friends wer endeavouring a mediation betuixt them, the pannall's expressions severall tymes wer that all was to no purpose, the sword behoved to decyde it; that since the murder he wished he wer but twenty yeeres of age again, which, if he wer, he should make the Farquharsons besouth the Cairn of Month thinner, and should have a lyff for ilk finger and toe of his two dead sones." As to Mr Angus, "he houndit out" the others to the pursuit, and said to his sister, when lamenting the loss of her brothers, "She had no reason to lament for them, since they hade gott the lyff they wer seeking."

The trial of both parties took place on various days from the 2d to the 11th of June 1673. On the one side, John M'Comie of Forter, pursuer, "for himself, and in name and behalf of the rem-

nant kin and freinds of the saids John and Robert
M'Intoshes." The others named on the side of
the M'Comies were, James, Alexander, and Mr
Angus, sons; Thomas Fleyming, in Dalinamer,
John Burn, David Guthrie, Donald M'Intosh,
and Donald Gerters, tenants and servants — in
all ten persons, besides John M'Comie, senior.

On the other side, Helen Ogilvie, relict of the
deceased Robert Farquharson of Broughdearg;
Alexander Farquharson, his brother; James, Alexander, and John Farquharsons, his uncles, "for
themselves, and in name," &c., were pursuers.
The others named on the side of the Farquharsons were: "John Barnot, in Dunmae; Donald
M'Vadenach, in Burghderg; George Patton, ser-
vitor to Burghderg; Thomas M'Nicol, also servant; Duncan M'Coul of Kero; Thomas Creighton, in Milnetoun of Glenila; Alexander Farquharson, in Belnaboth; John Farquharson, in Belnaboth; John Farquharson of Dunnieday; James
Farquharson, in Milne of Ingzeon; William Farquharson, his sone; John Farquharson, in Cantsmilne; —— Farquharson, his sone." In all, in-

cluding, as in the case of the M'Comies, the two slain, eighteen persons.

The result of the trial as regards the main charges—viz., the deaths near the Moss of Forfar —was that each of the pursuers abandoned their case, both parties seeing that to follow the double action to the end would only be to bring several of the survivors on both sides under the severest penalty of the law. We have already seen that of those on the M'Comies' side, James M'Comie and Alexander M'Comie, his sons, and Donald Gerters, John Burn, and David Guthrie, his servants, were outlawed as fugitives. On the 9th June, Duncan M'Coul of Kero; Thomas Creighton, in Milnetoun of Glenila; John Farquharson, in Cantsmilne; —— Farquharson, his son, "being ofttymes called," for their share of the raids of Crandart and Kilulock, and the three last mentioned for killing the wounded John M'Comie, and having been duly summoned, and "not enterand and compeirand," the Lords Commissioners of Justiciary "decerned and adjudged the haill forenamed persones to be denunced our Soveragne Lord's rebells, and ordained them to be put to the horne, and all ther movable goods and gear to be escheat and inbrought to his Majesties use, as fugitives frae the lawes, for the crymes above specified—which wes pronunced for doome." [1]

That the Farquharsons had now enough of the feud which they themselves had originated, and been the agressors in, and were now in dread of the old chief whom they had thought to have subdued, is evident from the fact that, on the same day on which the several actions were abandoned by both parties, " Helen Ogilvie, relict of the deceast Robert Farquharson of Brughderg, craved law - burrowes of the said Johne M'Intosh of Forther, and made faith that she dreadit him bodylie harme and oppression;" whereupon the Lords Commissioners ordered him to find caution. " In obedience whereof the said John M'Intosh, as principall, and Thomas Oliver, of Westmiln, in Glenila, and Thomas M'Intosh, merchant in Montrose, as cautioner and sovertie

[1] Appendix, Note N.

for him, gave caution, in form according to Act of Parliament." Item, 16th June: "Thomas Fleyming, in Dalinamer in Glenila, was set at libertie, upon caution to appear on 15 days' notice." He had stood prisoner with John M'Comie and his son, Mr Angus.[1]

And now, after a long and most eventful life, John M'Comie, *the* M'Comie Mor, died in peace, in his own house at Crandart, before 12th January 1676.[2] His sagacity and unconquerable spirit, his chivalrous courage and extraordinary personal strength, marked him out as a true leader of men in revolutionary times such as those in which he lived. That he was the most remarkable man of his time in the district in which he lived, is indisputably proved by his traditionary fame even at the present time. In few districts in Scotland has the memory of a man who died over two hundred years ago been kept living so vividly by tradition, as has that of M'Comie Mor, in Glenshee and Glenisla. He was buried in Glenisla churchyard, beside his two sons who were killed at Drum-

[1] Appendix, Note O. [2] Appendix, Note P.

gley. Not many years ago, the late Rev. Mr
Simpson, Free Church minister of Glenisla, told
the late Mr J. B. M'Combie, advocate, Aberdeen,
and great-great-great-grandson of M'Comie Mor,
that he was present in Glenisla churchyard,
when, in digging a grave in the spot pointed
out by tradition as the burying-place of the
M'Comies, some immense bones were exhumed,
which Mr Simpson and others who saw them
had no doubt were those of M'Comie Mor, or
one of his sons.

Of John M'Comie's seven sons, John and
Robert were killed, as already narrated. James,
who was outlawed in 1673, for not appearing to
stand his trial, on finding the main action departed from by both parties, returned, and had
doubtless had little trouble in getting the sen-
tence of outlawry reversed. Accordingly we find
that, on the 12th January 1676, " Jacobus M'Intosh de Forther " was served nearest lawful heir
to Robert M'Intosh, his younger brother, who
had been portioner of Gambok, in four acres of
arable land of the town and lands of Easter-

Denhead, near Coupar - Angus (which he had
doubtless inherited from his mother's family), in
the field called Cottarbank ; in the piece of un-
laboured ground at Corshill; and with common
pasturage in the Soidmyre.[1]   From the same
source[2] we learn that Thomas M'Comie, son of
John M'Intosh, *alias* M'Comie, of Forther, was
served nearest heir to the foregoing James, his
elder brother, on January 2, 1677.   Of Mr
Angus, the late Mr William Shaw, of Milton of
Blacklunans, in the letter already quoted from,
says that James M'Intosh, there referred to, "told
me that it was an Angus M'Comie, *alias* M'Intosh, that restored Forter to the Airlie family ;
that this is seen in the process between Sir David
Wedderburn of Ballindean and the Airlies."
From the 'Registrum Magni Sigilli,' lib. lxix.
No. 51, it appears that there was a charter under
the Great Seal, of date 15th December 1682,
granting to Alexander M'Intosh the lands of
Wester Innerharitie, in the parish of Glenisla,

---

[1] Inquisitionum Retornatarum Abbreviatio, vol. ii. p. 1125, 1811.
[2] *Ibid.*, vol. ii. p. 5962.

and sheriffdom of Forfar. Alexander, it will be remembered, had been outlawed with James in 1673. There remains now only the youngest son, Donald, from whom are descended the well-known M'Combies of Aberdeenshire, and whose history we now proceed to take up.

But before doing so, let us take a last look at Crandart, where, on the death of M'Comie Mor, and the subsequent dispersion of his family, the fortunes of the M'Comies seemed for ever wrecked. Of the old Ha' of Crandart little remains. The outlines of the old house can still be made out as regards the ground-plan, and the sides of the door and one window of the present farmhouse, and another in the steading, with their moulded corners, and the threshold-stone, were taken from the old Ha'. Besides these stones, there are two stones with inscriptions still left from the old mansion-house. One of these is built into the south end of the west wing of the present steading at Crandart. On it is the following inscription :—

I · M ·   ♡   E · C ·

I♢I   I♢I

·TIE · LORD · DEFEND · TIIS · FAMILI(E)·

16   60

The other stone was, unwarrantably we believe, removed from Crandart, first to Dal-na-Sneachd, across the Isla, and from thence to Balharry, where it now is. The inscription on it is—

I SIIALL · OVERCOM · INVY · VITI

GODS · IIELP · TO · GOD · BE · AL ·

PRAIS · IIONOVR · AND · GLORIE

16   60

At Balharry it possesses little interest for any one, and we think it a great pity it was ever removed from Crandart. At Crandart it would be in its original home, and would be a silent memento of him who placed it there—the hero in tradition and history, of Glenshee and Glenisla, M'Comie Mor.

F

CHAPTER III.

IT is easy to see that many events from 1660
to 1673 had tended to exhaust the resources
and weaken the position of the M'Comies. The
litigation with Lord Airlie concerning the right
of free forestry in Canlochan, terminating in two
Acts and Decrees of the Scottish Parliament
in Lord Airlie's favour, must have cost John
M'Comie much money, as he, in that and the
subsequent trials, employed the best counsel of
his time. The loss of the forest itself as a
grazing and hunting ground, when at last given
up, must have caused a serious diminution of

income. Then, again, the legal conflict with
Lord Airlie was almost immediately followed by
the exaction of the Government fine of £1800, a
very large sum in those times. Although there
are substantial grounds for believing that the
bond granted to the Farquharsons, under the
circumstances already narrated, was never paid,
yet the resistance of its payment must have
entailed very considerable law costs. All this,
followed by the great trial in 1673, must have
reduced the fortunes of the family to a very low
ebb. We have seen that the old chief did not
long survive this; and the facts relating to the
history of the family for some time afterwards
are very meagre. There can be little doubt
but that the property was burdened by debt ere
this time,[1] and that the surviving sons of John
M'Comie, finding it impossible to make headway
longer at home, one by one set out in search of
better fortune. Of the subsequent fortunes of
those who remained south of the Grampians we
have no authentic record, and the history of the

[1] Appendix, Note Q.

M'Comies must now be transferred from Perth
and Forfar to Aberdeenshire, where the youngest son, Donald M'Comie, settled, while still a
very young man, towards the end of the seventeenth century. The date of the migration of
Donald M'Comie from Glenisla to the vale of
Alford is not known exactly, but was probably
between 1676 and 1680, as by the Poll-book
for Aberdeenshire of date 1696, we find him
married to Janet Shires, and tenant to the yearly
value of £10 in a holding at Edindurnoch, now
Nethertown of Tough. In addition to his poll-
tax as tenant, he was taxed six shillings additional
as a tradesman. From this it is evident that he
had been a considerable time in Aberdeenshire
previous to 1696. There can be little doubt but
that, owing to the circumstances above mentioned,
and from his being the youngest son, he brought
little into Aberdeenshire except a few personal
effects. There has always been a tradition that
he brought a few relics with him from Crandart,
which have, unfortunately, not been preserved in
the family. Looking back on the circumstances

of Donald M'Comie in 1696, they are about as unpropitious as could be; and the subsequent slow but steady rise of the family in fortune and influence, through no sudden accession of fortune, but by steady unremitting perseverance and prudence, is of itself sufficient proof that its fortunes were laid by a race of men who, however impeded they might be by adverse circumstances for a time, could rise superior to all ill-fortune, if unconquerable will and strength of purpose could effect it.

Of the personal history of Donald M'Comie little has come down to the present time, his life having evidently been one of uninterrupted industry, free from any remarkable incident. From the parish records of Tough we gather that he was frequently employed as a valuator, which shows that he had come to be looked upon as a man of sound judgment, and to be held in considerable reputation. Before his death he became tenant in Mains of Tonley, in Tough, where he died in 1714. His stone[1] in

[1] Appendix, Note R.

the churchyard of Tough is amongst the oldest, if not the oldest one in it with an inscription. There is a tradition that when the people of Tough were visited by the cateran, Donald M'Comie sometimes got these troublesome visitors away with as little loss as possible to the community, not, as his father, "big M'Comie in the head of the Lowlands," used to do, by the terror of his sword, but by his persuasive words addressed to them in Gaelic. In Glenshee, the early home of his father, Gaelic was the ordinary language of everyday life, and is still spoken there, although we are sorry to say it is fast dying out. Donald M'Comie was therefore familiar with it, and all who know the Highlanders know how their heart warms to any one who can address them in their own tongue, especially when they meet with one who speaks it where they believe it is unknown. It is not difficult to understand, therefore, how he came to have such influence with the wild cateran.

Donald's son Robert became tenant in Findlatrie, also in Tough, and overlooking Lynturk. His life seems to have been spent like that of his

father, in peaceful industry, which was soon to
bear fruit, as the rapid rise of the family after
his time is evidence that he was laying a good
foundation on which his descendants could raise
a lasting superstructure. He married Isobel
Ritchie, daughter of Mr Ritchie, Farmton of
Alford. One of his sons, Robert, was out in
1745, and in 1746 escaped with difficulty from
the rout of Culloden. After the battle he was
overtaken by three dragoons, of whom he asked
and fortunately obtained quarter. Scarcely, however, were they out of sight when a single dra-
goon overtook him, and on his refusing quarter,
Robert M'Combie drew his pistol and shot the
horse, and after a brief combat slew the rider.
After this he managed to get home in safety,
and after spending some time in concealment,
succeeded in getting first to Whitehaven in
England, and subsequently went to the West
Indies, where his future history is unknown.

The eldest son of Robert was William, grandfather of the present proprietor of Easterskene
and Lynturk. He became tenant of Upper and
Lower Farmton and Mains of Lynturk in 1748,

residing at Lynturk, where his house still remains, with the date 1762 on the lintel above the door. It is situated close to the present mansion-house of Lynturk, and the stones round the doors and windows, with their moulded corners, very like those at Crandart, were taken from the old castle of Lynturk, which was situated a little to the north-west. The present proprietor re-members seeing his grandfather in this house, which is a relic of great interest to him, and has been recently new-roofed to preserve the walls.

A most interesting fact in connection with the history of the M'Combies has been the hered-itary transmission uninterruptedly for over 500 years of great personal stature and strength. The seventh chief of the M'Intoshes, William, from whom they are descended, was a man " of stature exceeding that of common men." The M'Comie who got the charter for Finnegand had the cognomen of *Mor* in 1571, and although John M'Comie of Forter was *the* M'Comie Mor *par excellence* in legend and history, it must be

remembered that his ancestors had the same cognomen before him, and his son John, who was
slain at the Moss of Forfar, was known as young
M'Comie Mor. So little of the personal history
of Donald and Robert has come down to us,
that we find no particular record of their personal
appearance; but no sooner do we come to learn
particulars of the personal appearance of their descendants than this hereditary personal characteristic is as marked as ever. The late George
Mackie, slater, who was when young a servant to
William M'Combie at Lynturk, used to tell the
present proprietor of Lynturk that his grandfather
at Lynturk had the largest bones of any man he
ever met with, and he had the reputation of being
the strongest man of seven parishes. His son
Thomas, the present proprietor's father, used to
be the champion putter of the stone on the links
of Aberdeen, among the young men of his time.
His eldest son, "the stalwart laird" of Easterskene, is 6 ft. 2 in., and very muscular; and his
brother, the late Mr J. B. M'Combie, was also
6 ft. 2 in., and of massive build. Their cousin,

the late Dr M'Combie of Tillyfour, was about the same height. James M'Combie of Farmton was a remarkably strong man. Charles M'Combie of Tillychetly, the father of the present tenant, was a powerfully built deep-chested man; and many will remember the tall figure of the late editor of the 'Free Press.' In very few families has a personal characteristic been transmitted in so conspicuous a manner for such a length of time—over 500 years, dating from William, seventh chief of the M'Intoshes.

William M'Combie, when a young man, was, like his great ancestor, distinguished for his personal prowess. Up to the beginning of the present century, and in many instances well into it, faction fights between the inhabitants of different parishes or districts were very common in Aberdeenshire, and, we believe, all over the country. A remarkable fight of this kind took place when William M'Combie was a young man, on the occasion of a penny, or, as it was sometimes called, a "siller" wedding between a Leochel man and a Monymusk woman. On this occasion the fight that took place seems to have been between not only the guests present from the parishes of Leochel and Monymusk, but also those from several neighbouring parishes, the combatants ranging themselves with the bridegroom's party or the bride's, according to residence west or east respectively of Cairn William. William M'Combie was captain of the Leochel or west of Cairn William men, and a noted fighting man named Thomson from Mill of Hole, Midmar, captain of the Monymusk or east of Cairn William men. The fight was a long and stubborn one; and a vivid idea of the vigour with which it was prosecuted, and the hard knocks going, is conveyed by the fact that William M'Combie sent his youngest brother Donald to strip some neighbouring houses of their thatch, and bring the cabers to supply the necessary weapons of war for such of the Leochel men and their partisans as had the misfortune to break their own cudgels on the heads of their opponents. Victory is said to have rested ultimately with the bridegroom's party, in great measure owing to the prowess of their captain, who defeated the Midmar champion in single combat.

On another occasion William M'Combie had gone into a neighbouring parish to attend a ball, at which there was present a young man with whom he had had a quarrel, which had not been satisfactorily settled. As the night wore on he observed this young man consulting from time to time with several of his associates, and being suspicious of mischief being plotted against himself, he kept a wary eye on their movements. At length observing some commotion in the other end of the ball-room from where he was standing, he noticed that his opponent and his associates were making their way towards him, in a line extending from side to side of the house, so as to prevent his escape, while the women and the more peaceably inclined of the dancers were making a hurried exit. But like the athletic miller of " Christ's Kirk on the Green "—

> " *M'Comie* was o' manly mak,
>   To meet him was nae mows;
>   There durst nae tensome there him tak,
>   Sae noited he ther pows "—

for springing upwards he wrenched a caber from the roof above him, and using it like a two - handed sword, with terrific sweeps right and left he cleared the ball-room and escaped without injury.

His strength and courage on occasions such as these, made him very popular amongst the young men of the surrounding district, a popularity that was like to have brought him into some trouble in 1745. The proprietor of Tonley at that time was an ardent supporter of Prince Charles, and became active in raising men in his behalf. Well knowing William M'Combie's personal prowess, and his popularity among the class of men he wanted to join the Prince's army, he was sure that if he got him to join, many would follow his example, while if he held back, many would probably do the same who would otherwise have joined. William M'Combie's father being a tenant of Tonley, the laird made sure of getting any of his tenant's sons he wanted, and as we have seen, did get Robert, but found William determined to have nothing to do with him or Prince Charlie; perhaps the memory of what his family had already suffered from taking a side in civil war had something to do with his refusal. Tonley, finding persuasion of no avail, determined to carry him off by force, thinking that if he were once away and amongst the others engaged in the enterprise, he would not like to turn back. Tonley's wife, however, secretly conveyed word to young M'Combie of the design of her husband, and when the latter went with a strong party to carry him off, he could not be found. It is said that William M'Combie looked upon Tonley, who had not been long in possession of the estate, as a *novus homo* who was trying to acquire prestige for himself at the expense of others, and on that account was less inclined to join him.

After entering on his tenancy at Lynturk, William M'Combie came to care less and less for distinguishing himself as the hero of such scenes as we have narrated, and a rather remarkable incident that happened to him while there had a permanent influence on his after-life.

About this time there were a considerable number of Dissenters in the district around Lynturk; and before there was a manse for their pastor, the latter was for some time lodged with William M'Combie at Lynturk, although he had not at that time joined himself to the Dissenters. One day while William M'Combie was in one of his fields, he heard a voice proceeding from behind a dike at some distance. Drawing near he became aware that it was his lodger engaged in prayer, and was greatly moved on finding that special entreaty was being made for his own spiritual welfare. The result was that soon after he joined himself to the Dissenters, and became their leading member in the congregation at Buffle. This connection has been maintained by some of his sons and their descendants down to the present time in the U.P. congregation at Lynturk, which now represents the Buffle one.

William M'Combie, after settling at Lynturk, married Marjory Wishart, daughter of Mr Wishart, merchant, Banchory, by whom he had a family of seven sons and three daughters. The sons were Alexander, Robert, William, John, Thomas, Peter, and Charles. William's great-grandfather, it will be remembered, had seven sons also, and as in their time the fortunes of the family were at their lowest, so now, from amongst the seven sons of his descendant, they were once more to be restored to even more than their former position. Four of the seven names, it will be observed, correspond with the names of four of the former family of seven sons. The names of William's seven sons, contracted in the usual Scottish fashion, formed a sort of anapestic rhythm, as follows: Sănĭe, Rōb, Wĭllĭe, Jōck, Tăm, Păte, and Chārlĭe,—at one time very popular amongst scholars in the parishes of Tough and Leochel, and still remembered by many who never knew, or have forgotten the origin of it.

Alexander, the eldest son, was a man of great size and strength of body, but lacked energy of mind, and was content to reside with his brother Robert at Upper Farmton, where he lived and died unmarried.

Robert, the second son, was tenant of Upper and Lower Farmton, and married a daughter of Mr Milner, Mains of Corse. His eldest son, William, became tenant in turn of Upper Farmton, and had four sons: William, who died young; Peter and James, both deceased; and Robert, the present tenant of Upper Farmton. Robert's second son, James, became tenant of Lower Farmton, and had a son, Robert, who died young; and a daughter, married to John Hunter, till recently farmer in Lower Farmton, whose daughter is married to Dr M'Donald of Markinch, Fife; Jessie, the sister of the present tenant of Upper Farmton, unmarried; and Helen, married to Mr Duffus, whose son is now tenant of Lower Farmton, brings the family of William down to the present time, and leaves them tenants of Lower and Upper Farmton, as his father had been. The daughters of the first Robert of Farmton were Marjory, married to Mr Smith, Easter Tolmands, whose son is the present tenant there; and Penelope, who had no family.

William, the third son, became tenant of the

G

Netherton of Tough, where his great-grandfather Donald M'Combie first settled, and married a Miss Urquhart. Their son William was their successor in Netherton, where he died not many years ago. Their son Charles became tenant of Tillychetly in the parish of Alford, now tenanted by his son Charles. Their daughter was married to her cousin William in Upper Farmton.

John, the fourth son, held a situation in the Customs, Aberdeen, the family ultimately settling in London.

Thomas, the fifth son, was born in 1762, and became a merchant in Aberdeen, of which he was a magistrate, being several times a bailie and member of the town council, and refused the honour of the provostship. His success in business enabled him to buy the estate of Jellybrands in the end of the last century, and the estates of Asleid and Easterskene in the beginning of the present century. He was the first of the M'Combies north of the Grampians who succeeded in regaining the position held by his

ancestors in Perthshire and Forfarshire as land-
owners. It is doubtless owing to this circumstance in great part that his eldest son, the present
proprietor of Easterskene and Lynturk, has been
looked upon as the chief of the name, it being
a well-known fact that the chieftainship of Highland clans did not always go by seniority of birth
or direct succession. Thomas married Margaret
Boyn, daughter of Mr Boyn of the Customs,
Aberdeen, by whom he had a family of three
sons and five daughters, of whom two died young.
He died in 1824, and was succeeded in Easterskene by his eldest son William, born in 1802,
whose biography will be given later on. Mr
James Boyn M'Combie, his second son, succeeded
by destination to the estate of Jellybrands, and
had a long and honourable career as an advocate
in Aberdeen. He was much esteemed by his
townsmen of Aberdeen, and but for his retiring
disposition would have been brought more prom-
inently into public life than was the case. As
it was, he was Dean of Guild once; and his popularity for the provostship on one occasion was

set forth in song in one of the newspapers, one
verse of which was as follows :—

> "Oh wha's to be provost? wha? wha?
> Oh wha's to be provost? wha?
> Ye should tak Jellybrands,
> He's made to your hands;
> He's a dungeon of wit, and of law, law,
> He's a dungeon of wit, and of law."

He married Miss Helen Davidson, daughter of
Mr Davidson of Elmsfield, but had no family.
He died in 1885.

Thomas, the third son, inherited Asleid and
Richmond Hill. He married Miss Catherine
Arbuthnot, daughter of Mr Robert Arbuthnot
of Mount Pleasant, and left an only daughter,
Nicola, married to Mr Thomas Hutchison, who
held a situation in the National Debt Office for
many years : issue, two sons and two daughters.

The daughters of Mr Thomas M'Combie of
Easterskene were Barbara, married to Dr Alexander Ewing of Tartowie, a very successful
physician and surgeon in Aberdeen, whose only
surviving son is Major Alexander Ewing of the
Army Pay Department, who married Juliana

Horatia Gatty, a well-known author. Thomas
M'Combie's second daughter was Margaret, married to Mr Simpson Duguid of Cammachmore,
whose son, Mr Peter Duguid of Cammachmore,
advocate, married Miss Adamson, daughter of
Mr Adamson, merchant and shipowner, Aberdeen : issue, two sons and a daughter.

Isabella, the third daughter, was married to
Mr David Blaikie, of Blaikie Brothers, whose
only son John married a daughter of General
Tweedie of East India Company's service : issue,
one son and two daughters. The daughters were :
Margaret, married to Mr Patrick Keith, of the
firm of Gladstone, Wylie, & Co.—issue, two sons
and four daughters ; Helen, married first to Mr
Hislop, Prestonpans, second to Major Wood, 91st
Highlanders, third to Mr Williamson.

Peter, sixth son of William M'Combie, Lynturk,
like his brother Thomas, engaged successfully in
business in Aberdeen, and early in the present
century bought the barony of Lynturk, on which
his father had been tenant so long, and where
he and his brothers had been born and brought

up.   He married Miss Murray, daughter of Rev.
Mr Murray, minister at Buffle, but left no issue,
his nephew Mr William M'Combie of Easterskene succeeding to the property.

Charles, the seventh son, became proprietor of
Tillyfour, which, in the hands of his son, was to
become a household word in the agricultural
world.   He married Miss Ann Black, daughter
of a Buchan farmer of good position, and had a
large family, several of whom died young.   He
was well known over the north of Scotland as a
worthy, upright gentleman, and a successful cattle-
dealer on a very extensive scale.   He was succeeded as proprietor of Tillyfour by his eldest
son Charles, who, for the long period of forty-
nine years, was minister of Lumphanan.   He
received the degree of LL.D. from the University of Aberdeen, and few men have ever led a
more unblemished life, or approached nearer to
the ideal of a perfect Christian gentleman.   He
died at Lumphanan in 1874.   He was married
first to Miss Scott, daughter of the Rev. Robert
Scott, minister of Glenbucket, by whom he had

one son, deceased ; second, to Miss Eliza Lamond, daughter of Mr Lamond of Pitmurchie,
by whom he had four sons and five daughters, of
whom only three survive, — Thomas, in Cape
Colony, unmarried ; Isabella, married to the
Rev. Mr Young, Ellon ; and Rachel, unmarried.

William M'Combie, the second son, will be
noticed further on.

Thomas, the third son, who reached maturity,
emigrated to Australia, where he had a prosperous and honoured career, being elected a
member of the Legislative Council of Victoria.
He came home to settle in the old country, but
did not long survive. He left a widow and two
daughters, who are both married. The daughters
of Charles of Tillyfour who reached maturity were
Marjory, married to the Rev. Mr Laing, Aberdeen ; and Mary, married first to Mr P. C. Auld,
the well-known artist—issue, three sons ; second,
to the Rev. Mr Forbes, Oban.

The daughters of William M'Combie in Lynturk, were Isobel, unmarried ; Helen, married to

Mr Dunn, merchant, Aberdeen, who had no issue; and Marjory, married to her cousin, William M'Combie in Cairnballoch, whose son William had a very successful career as a journalist and author. It was under his management that the 'Aberdeen Free Press' was started, which under his care and editing attained a distinguished position amongst the provincial press, which it has fully maintained to the present time under his successors. He was also the author of 'Hours of Thought' and several other well-known works, which met with a large share of public favour. He was a self-made man, having attained his success in life through his natural talents and perseverance. He left a large family of sons and daughters, who have also shown marked ability.

We must now go back again to the time of William M'Combie, Lynturk, and briefly notice the other two sons of Robert M'Combie, Findlatrie, Donald and Alexander. Donald became farmer in Boghead, Tough, and left an only daughter, married to Mr Moses Copland, also farmer there, as were their descendants for some time. Alexander was a litstar at Bandley. His daughter, Grizel M'Combie, was married to Mr Alexander Garden, in Bandley, among their family being Mr George Garden, also in Bandley, and Colonel William Garden of the East India Company's service. Mr George Garden, Bandley, had a son, the well-known Dr William Garden, in Balfluig, Alford, who had a son, Mr Farquharson Taylor Garden.

The daughter of Robert M'Combie in Findlatrie, was married to Mr Reid, Cromore, Craigmyle; issue, one son, Robert; issue, a daughter.

CHAPTER IV.

WILLIAM M'COMBIE of Tillyfour, the second son of Charles M'Combie of Tillyfour, was born in 1805. As it was his father's wish that he, with his elder brother, should enter one of the learned professions, he was sent to Aberdeen University; but the result of two sessions at Marischal College was so un-satisfactory that his father took him home and set him to work a pair of horses. In after-life,

he often regretted his neglect of education in
early life ; and the higher the position he attained,
the more he felt the disadvantages of that neglect.
The only good result that came of this neglect
was the benefit acquired by practical experience
of a ploughman's work.   This he held to be in-
valuable for every one who intended to follow
agriculture in its widest sense as a profession.
His ideal of the training necessary for a farmer's
life was, first, a good education, especially in all
that was likely to be of practical use afterwards,
laying particular stress on English grammar and
composition ;   second, a practical training in all
kinds of farm-work—not a turn now and then as
a pastime, but filling the place of a regular work-
man for a stipulated time.   After that preliminary
training, a man was fit to enter on the superintendence of work, and ready to acquire experience
in buying and selling stock, and to exercise his
judgment generally on everything pertaining to
practical farming.

After two years' probation as a ploughman, the
future "Grazier King" began some dealing on

his own account, some details of which are given
in his 'Cattle and Cattle-Breeders.' Previous to
his father's death, he became tenant of the home
farm of Tillyfour, including Tillyreach and Nether-
hill—a tenancy continued during the lifetime of
his brother, who had been settled as minister of
Lumphanan some time before his father's death.
Some years afterwards he became tenant of Bridgend, on the estate of Lynturk—a tenancy only
broken by his own death. Still later he became
tenant of Dorsell in Alford, which he held until
he purchased Tillyfour. From about 1830 he
was free to follow his own bent in regard to
cattle, yet there was no systematic attempt at
cattle-breeding until some fourteen or fifteen
years afterwards. Until this later period, he
was rather of a sporting turn, and was a good
shot and a capital horseman. His shooting he
continued occasionally up to about 1856. As
a rider he performed many astonishing feats,
being always well mounted, and covering extraordinary distances to and from markets on one
horse in one day. To the last he liked to see

a good fast horse, and had many horses in his time well known for their high powers of speed and endurance. He also engaged in coursing at one time, and once won and once divided the all-aged stakes at Turriff with Amy, whose portrait held a conspicuous place in the dining-room at Tillyfour. During this period, 1830-45, with the exception of an odd beast now and then sent to Alford shows, his breeding stock was composed of ordinary country cows kept for dairy purposes, the lean cattle trade being still his main dependence; and not until 1844 or 1845 did he enter on the main work of his life—the breeding and improvement of the polled Aberdeen-Angus breed of cattle. From that time onwards he devoted the best energies of his life to that object. With good abilities and good opportunities, a man who determines to follow out a certain aim in life is sure of success if granted time; and William M'Combie had rare abilities, good opportunities, and had over thirty years of uninterrupted application of his abilities and opportunities. The result was a success altogether without parallel. When he commenced the breeding of Aberdeen-Angus polled cattle, the breed had not long been shown as a distinct class at shows. At that time there were at least three breeds of cattle—shorthorns in England and Scotland, and Herefords and Devons in England—whose supporters would have derided the idea of serious rivalry from the Scottish black polls of Aberdeen and Angus, while several other breeds were at least on an equality with them. Yet in little over twenty years from starting in earnest to improve the breed, William M'Combie both bred and fed a pure polled Aberdeen-Angus ox that put completely into the shade the best shorthorns, Herefords, and Devons that Great Britain could produce; and twelve years later, in a competition open to the world, he took first place with the same breed, beating every other breed of note either at home or abroad.

From the time he entered on this work, it became the main business of his life. He was never at rest long from Tillyfour. When necessarily absent on business, he always set out for home immediately it was finished. Every day of his life, if at home and well, he made his rounds of his byres or his fields, and saw every beast; and no eye was quicker in detecting anything amiss with any of them. Such unremitting ardour soon brought success, show-yard honours came thick and fast, and what is more, continued. The agricultural world began to realise that this was no common man, making lucky hits now and again, but a man with a genius for what he had taken in hand—a man making history in his own particular walk of life.

In recognition, therefore, of the work he was accomplishing, he was entertained to dinner at Aberdeen in 1862 by about four hundred of the leading noblemen and gentlemen in the north of Scotland connected with agriculture, under the presidency of the late Marquis of Huntly. On that occasion he, in a few words, put before the public what had been his aim in life, and to what extent he had attained it. " I was led," said he, " by a father whose memory I revere, to believe that our polled cattle are peculiarly suited to our

soil and climate, and that if their properties were
rightly brought out, they would equal, if not sur-
pass, any other breed as to weight, symmetry,
and quality of flesh.   I resolved that I would
endeavour to improve our native breed.   I exerted all my energies to accomplish this purpose.
For many years I was an unsuccessful exhibitor
at the Smithfield Club.   I went to Baker Street.
I minutely examined the prize-winners.   I di-
rected my attention especially to the points in
which the English were superior to the Scottish
cattle.   I came to the conclusion that I had been
beaten, not because our Scottish breed was in-
ferior to the English breeds,—I saw that I had
been beaten because I was imperfectly acquainted
with the points of the animals most appreciated
in Baker Street.   I doubled, I tripled, I quad-
rupled the cake allowed to my feeding stock.   I
attained the object of my ambition.   English
agriculturists always maintained that a Scot would
never take a first place in a competition with a
shorthorn, a Hereford, or a Devon.   I have
given them reason for changing their opinion."

Not long after this he was entertained to dinner by the farm-servants and tradesmen of the vale of Alford, an honour which he always looked back upon with especial pride. In 1865, when the rinderpest was paralysing stock-breeders by its ravages, the farmers of Aberdeenshire, under the leadership of William M'Combie, showed the agricultural world how to grapple successfully with this evil, by the stamping-out process they adopted.

In 1866 he succeeded Mr George Hope, Fentonbarns, as second president of the Scottish Chamber of Agriculture. In December of the following year his fortunes as a combined feeder and breeder of the polled Aberdeen-Angus cattle reached a climax, when Black Prince, a pure Aberdeen-Angus ox bred and fed by himself, was, Eclipse-like, "first, and the rest nowhere," both at Birmingham and London. So conspicuous was he by his superiority over all the most noted English breeds, that her Majesty the Queen expressed a wish to see so notable an animal. He was accordingly sent by Windsor on his way from Birmingham to London. Her Majesty was greatly struck with the magnificent black, and Mr M'Combie was so proud of the honour done to himself through his champion, that, after Smithfield, he offered the Black Prince as a gift to his sovereign. Her Majesty of course declined so large a present, but graciously accepted the baron of beef for her Christmas dinner. The after-result of this was, that Mr M'Combie had the high honour of receiving her Majesty at Tillyfour in 1868. On this occasion some 400 polled cattle were spread over the fields surrounding the mansion-house of Tillyfour, in which her Majesty took tea before setting out on her return to Balmoral.

In 1867 'Cattle and Cattle-Breeders,' by William M'Combie, Tillyfour, was published. Few men seemed more unlikely at one time to have turned author than he was. 'Cattle and Cattle-Breeders' was, however, a success, going through three editions in a few years. It contained much valuable matter on the breeding, feeding, and care of cattle, and some racy reminiscences of the great cattle-dealers in the beginning of the century. The style is plain and unaffected, being just such as a man adopts who, without any pretensions to literary culture, has something to say, and says it in a simple, straightforward manner. For its *raison d'être* the book supplied a good deal of information, not before published, on matters of moment to an important part of the community, which is more than can be said of most books.

Although now over sixty years of age, and held in honour by all classes, from sovereign to peasant, William M'Combie was yet looking forward, in 1867, to still further honours in a new field. When it became certain that the county of Aberdeen was to have an additional member of Parliament as soon as the Reform Bill of 1867 became law, he diligently canvassed West Aberdeenshire, and at the general election in 1868 he was returned unopposed, being the first tenant-farmer returned for a Scottish constituency, and the second returned to the House of Commons. As a member of Parliament, he had the ear of the House of Commons whenever he spoke on agricultural questions, and the unwavering confidence of his constituents. At the general election in 1874 he was opposed by Mr Edward Ross, more celebrated as a rifle-shot than as a politician. The result was the most decisive victory obtained by any member returned at that election, the figures being — M'Combie, 2401 ; Ross, 326.

There can be no doubt, however, but that his parliamentary duties, coupled with his large farming operations, and the management of his famous breeding - herd, put too great a strain on his powers. When, therefore, after his brother's death, he, in 1875, purchased Tillyfour, it was not to be wondered at that he gave up Dorsell, the most outlying of his farms from Tillyfour, in that year, and resigned his parliamentary duties in 1876. On the occasion of his retirement, a large sum of money was subscribed for, and invested so as to provide the " M'Combie Prize" annually at Aberdeen for the best specimen of the breed with which his name was so indissolubly connected. Thus honoured, and lightened of part of his work, he settled down more closely to his home affairs, and projected many improvements on the home farm and estate of Tillyfour, several of which he saw effected. But he was failing fast in bodily strength. Those long reckless rides, at all times and in all weathers, when in the heyday of his youth and strength, were having their effect now. But before the end he was to have one crowning honour and glory for the breed he had done so much for. In 1878, at the great Exhibition at Paris, he won the two great prizes of the show against all the most famous breeds from every country of Europe, his group of polled Aberdeen-Angus cattle being first both for breeding and feeding qualities. It was a fitting close to a glorious career. Practically there was no further honour possible of acquirement for the Tillyfour herd. After this he was not long spared, and died, full of years and honours, at Tillyfour on February 1, 1880.

In this brief summary of the chief events of the life of William M‘Combie of Tillyfour, but

little idea can be formed of the man as he lived
and moved at home and abroad.   He was considerably above the average height, his personal
appearance being more indicative of strength and
vigour than of elegance or refinement.   His head
was massive, with a commanding forehead; the
rest of his features plain.   The disposition which
led him to neglect his education when young, also
led him to be less refined in speech and manners
than most people would have expected from the
high position he attained latterly in social life.
But his strength of intellect and force of will gave
a natural dignity to him, which did much to over-
shadow these defects, and no one could see him
without recognising a man born with power to
overcome obstacles, and to make a name for himself.   His neglect of education had also much to
do with his defects as an orator; yet here, again,
his force of character commanded attention, and
through the halting sentences his meaning would
come out clear and forcible in a few terse, homely
words.   Some of his unprepared speeches, had
they been printed *verbatim*, would have seemed

not much clearer than Cromwell's, yet, like him, ideas pregnant with meaning could be seen struggling through the seeming confusion and repetition.

As an agriculturist in the strict meaning of the word, he stood high. He reclaimed much on Tillyfour from heather and bog, pointing out with satisfaction fields great part of which he had himself ploughed for the first time. He dealt liberally in manure, employed only the best seeds, and took many prizes both for grain and root crops. He was very particular as to having good workmen, and it may safely be said that better ploughed and drilled fields, or better - built stacks, were not to be seen anywhere than on Tillyfour, Bridgend, and Dorsell. He was an excellent judge of men, and generally had a good idea of the worth of a man before he was long in his service. He had also a *penchant* for strong men, and was very proud of any of his servants who had won prizes at athletic sports, never failing to point them out to visitors, with a short history of their exploits. For a long period his three farms were training-schools for young men who wanted to push themselves on in the agricultural world, and he was ever willing to forward merit by generous recommendation. In the latter part of his life he paid strict attention to the duties of religion, holding family worship nightly with his immediate household, and on Sunday the whole of the servants at Tillyfour were assembled for this purpose. He was by no means ascetic, however, had a keen relish for humour, and enjoyed a hearty laugh. His outward demeanour was somewhat brusque and seemingly harsh at times, but those who knew him intimately, knew that there was much depth of kindly feeling beneath it. His success in life was entirely due to his own conspicuous abilities, and untiring persistence in the course he had entered on. He was a " powerful, pushing, and prosperous M'Combie," a veritable M'Comie Mor in his own line, a benefactor of his time whose name and fame will long survive.

CHAPTER V.

WILLIAM M'COMBIE, eldest son of
Thomas M'Combie of Easterskene, and
Margaret, daughter of James Boyn, Esq.,
Aberdeen, was born in Aberdeen in 1802,
and was made a free infant burgess of the
city in the same year, his father being a
magistrate at that time, and magistrates when
in office being entitled to have that privi-
lege conferred on their sons born during their
magistracy. When a boy of about five or six

years of age, he remembers being along with his parents on a visit to his grandfather at Lynturk, and seeing and talking to him not long before he died, which was in 1808. This was in the old house of Lynturk, already mentioned as having been built by his grandfather. When we remember that his grandfather was eighty-eight years of age when he died, and was therefore born only six years after the death of his grandfather Donald, who did not live to be a very old man, we see that very little is wanting from having the history of the stirring events that took place in the family of the M'Combies in Glenisla and Glenshee between 1660 and 1673, told by a contemporary, and in several cases an eyewitness of them, to his grandson, who in turn could have told them to his grandson, who is still alive. Or in other words, only a few years were wanting, from the present head of the family being the *second* who could have received the history of the raid of Crandart in 1669 by direct oral communication from one who was witness of and shared in the consternation and wrath in the old Ha' of Crandart amongst the family of M'Comie Mor, when the dastardly outrage became known on that eventful New Year's morning. As it is, it is very remarkable that Mr M'Combie is but the third to whom the history of events that took place over two hundred years ago may be said to have come, by direct oral tradition, from an eyewitness and participator in them.[1]

Mr M'Combie was educated in Aberdeen, and graduated at Marischal College in 1820. In 1822 he was one of a number of young gentlemen from Aberdeenshire who went to Edinburgh to participate in the rejoicings consequent on the visit of George IV. to Scotland. In 1824, on the death of his father, he succeeded to the estate of Easterskene, and commenced the series of improvements which, continued up to the present time, has wrought a change hard to realise by those unacquainted with the aspect of the estate in 1824. But while busy with improvements at Easterskene, there had arisen

[1] Appendix, Note S.

in his mind before this time an earnest desire
to investigate, and if possible throw additional
light on, the history of his ancestors in Perthshire and Forfarshire. Up to the time when
Mr M'Combie began his researches, the family
in Aberdeenshire had little but traditionary reminiscences of the history of their ancestors.
The leading facts, such as their being landed
proprietors in Glenshee in Perthshire, and latterly
in Glenisla in Forfarshire, and of the feud with
the Farquharsons, and the breaking up of the
family soon afterwards, were well known to all
Donald's descendants in Aberdeenshire. Mr
M'Combie remembers hearing the particulars
of the fight at the Moss of Forfar from his
father and uncles, long before he knew that all
the details were preserved in the Justiciary
Records. His grandfather William used to deal
to a considerable extent in cattle—in fact, was
paving the way for his still more renowned son
Charles, and grandson William, of Tillyfour,
in the same line. His business in that line
occasionally took him to Forfarshire, where

he met and in time became acquainted with
the Earl of Airlie of that time. Lord Airlie
was greatly interested when he became aware
that this Aberdeenshire farmer was a great-
grandson of the famous M'Comie Mor who had
obtained the wadset of the barony of Forter
from the Earl of Airlie in the time of Charles I.,
and had required two Acts of the Scottish Parliament to make him forego his claim of free
forestry in Canlochan. So interested was he
and pleased with William M'Combie—who, like
so many of the descendants of M'Comie Mor,
carried proof of the genuineness of his descent
in his own massive frame—that he more than
once intimated the pleasure it would give him
to see the M'Combies once more settled in Glenisla. All these reminiscences were eagerly
gathered and treasured up in the mind of the
young laird of Easterskene. And now, after
long years of push and progress by Donald's
descendants, there was at length one who had
at once both the time, and not only the incli-
nation but an enthusiastic desire, to trace back

the history of his ancestors. In 1827 he
determined to visit Glenisla and Glenshee.
Mr Martin, at that time minister of Glenisla, knowing Mr M'Combie to be a descendant
of M'Comie Mor, had previously made his
acquaintance, and on Mr Martin's invitation,
Glenisla manse was made his headquarters.
The two weeks he then spent in wandering
over the upper end of Glenisla and of Glenshee, he has always looked back upon as
amongst the most interesting and pleasant of
his life. Twice since then he has gone over
the same ground. In these later expeditions
he was accompanied at one time by his brother,
Mr J. B. M'Combie—at another time by Dr
Taylor, minister of Leochel-Cushnie, who was
well skilled in antiquarian lore. At the time
of Dr Taylor's visit, he made out with considerable certainty the ground-plan of the mansion-
house of Crandart erected by John M'Comie
in 1660. On each occasion Mr M'Combie found
much to interest him, and met with local gentlemen willing to help him in his researches. The

late Mr William Shaw, Finnegand, entered
with great zeal into the matter, and to him Mr
M'Combie was indebted for many interesting
facts in the history of the M'Combies, both historical and traditional. The late Mr Thomas
Shaw, Little Forter, Glenisla, on Mr M'Combie's
first visit was very friendly and attentive, and
by him Mr M'Combie was led to study the
etymology of the Gaelic names of places, with
the result that more than one Gaelic scholar
has been with difficulty persuaded that Mr
M'Combie could not speak Gaelic. It is rather
strange, too, that Mr Shaw, his first preceptor
in the etymology of Gaelic names, was also unable to speak Gaelic. Mr J. B. M'Combie was
from the first an active assistant in the search for
documentary evidence regarding the history of
the family, and little by little much that hitherto
rested on tradition in the family was established
as historically correct. The record of the great
double trial M'Comies *v.* Farquharsons, Farquharsons *v.* M'Comies, was a grand find; so
also were the two Acts and Decreets of the Scot-

tish Parliament settling the dispute between
Lord Airlie and John M'Comie as to Canlochan.
The search after authentic records of his ancestors was no transient pursuit, but has continued throughout a long life.

In 1831, Mr M'Combie married Katherine
Ann Buchan Forbes, eldest daughter of Major
Alexander Forbes of Inverernan. This lady was
a Forbes by descent on both sides, her mother
being a daughter of Duncan Forbes Mitchell, Esq.
of Thainston, second son of Sir Arthur Forbes
of Craigievar. In 1832 a son, Thomas, was born.
In the same year was built the present handsome
mansion-house of Easterskene, and a short time
previously Mr M'Combie had succeeded to the
barony of Lynturk, on the death of his uncle
Peter. For about three years, therefore, from
the birth of his son, it seemed as if nothing
was wanting to his happiness and good fortune.
But such remarkable felicity rarely lasts long in
this world. In 1835 the first blow came in the
death of his wife, and six years later the death of
his son seemed for a time to have left life almost

a blank. Both wife and son lie side by side in the churchyard of Skene, and the following epitaph closed for ever in this world the record of two lives, in whom for a season were placed the brightest hopes : " Within this enclosure are interred the remains of Katherine Ann Buchan Forbes, the wife of William M'Combie of Easterskene and Lynturk, and daughter of Major Alexander Forbes of Inverernan, who died on the 16th day of April 1835, in the 26th year of her age ; and of their son Thomas, who died on the 15th of September 1841, in the 10th year of his age."

From this period Mr M'Combie gave his time almost exclusively to the management of his estates, which we now proceed to describe. The estate of Easterskene lies wholly in the parish of Skene, the mansion-house being about 9 miles west from Aberdeen, about 4½ miles south of the Don, and about 6 miles north of the Dee. The length from north to south is fully 2 miles, the breadth from east to west about 1¼ mile. The estate is bounded on the north by the lands

I

of Skene and Kinellar, on the east by the lands
of Achronie and Kirkville, on the south by the
lands of Cairnie and Skene, and on the west by
the lands of Skene.   The elevation ranges from
under 300 ft. above sea-level on the north side
of the Loch of Skene, to a little over 700 ft. on
the summit of the wooded height south-east from
Drumstone.   When Mr M'Combie succeeded to
the estate, much of the low ground was an unreclaimed swamp, while much of the higher ground
was a bare heather moor.   Now it may safely
be said that there is not a square yard of waste
ground on the estate, all being either in a course
of rotation, in pasture, or under wood.   The farms
from south to north, all with good houses and
well fenced, are Lochhead, South Bank, Howemoss, Millbuie, North Bank, and Drumstone.
The main road from Aberdeen to Alford and
Strathdon passes through the south end of the
estate.   From this a branch goes north to Kirkton of Skene, from near which the east avenue
leads to the mansion-house.   From Kirkton of
Skene a road joins the main road near Lochhead.

From the main road again, another strikes north
by the Free church and school, and north-west
by South Bank and Line of Skene. From this
again, a little above the school, a branch goes
past the home farm of Easterskene, below which
the west avenue strikes off to the mansion-house.
This road is continued past the home farm by
Howemoss, Millbuie, and Drumstone, being a
thoroughfare to Kintore and the right bank of
the Don eastwards from Kintore. Drumstone,
on the high ground on the north of the estate,
receives its name from the stone on which the
laird of Drum rested on his way to the hard-
fought battle of Harlaw in 1411, and took a last
look backwards to the lands of Drum, with a
presentiment that he would never see them again.
The stone forms a sort of natural chair, and has
always been an object of interest to Mr M'Combie,
who many years ago had " Drum's Stone, Harlaw, 1411," inscribed on it. Besides the farms
mentioned, most of the village of Kirkton of
Skene is on Easterskene, with various tradesmen,
and a blacksmith's shop at Millbuie, and a saw-

mill at Lochhead. Reserving notice of the home
farm in the meantime, we come to the mansion-
house, a handsome building in the Elizabethan
style, surrounded by beautiful and well - kept
policies, the whole having a southern aspect.
The situation is delightful, the view truly magnificent. To the south and west the Loch of
Skene, with the woods of Skene and Dunecht,
make a fine foreground, backed by the Hill of
Fare. Farther west, the Forest of Corennie, and
Bennachaille overlooking Tillyfour, and beyond
these the mountains overlooking Cromar, conspicuous amongst them the massive crown of
Morven; then to the south the Grampians, beyond
the valley of the Dee, with Mount Battock and
Clochnaben, and the lesser heights sloping gradu-
ally to the North Sea,—form a prospect of which
the eye never wearies. As one emerges from the
woods surrounding the lawn on the west, the
Mither Tap of Bennachie, with the wooded
heights of Cairn William, are seen to the north-
west shutting in the vale of Alford. As you
ascend to Drumstone the prospect on all sides

enlarges, until on the summit you command the rich valley of the Don stretching away by Kintore and Inverurie, beyond which lies the district of the Garioch. From here, too, Callievar, beyond the vale of Alford, the Tap o' Noth, the Buck of the Cabrach, and in the dim distance Ben Avon, are seen. To the east and north-east the view is circumscribed by the hills of Brimmond, Elrick, and Tyrebagger; but even with this slight drawback the panorama is one of rare beauty and grandeur.

The barony of Lynturk is about 24 miles by road west of Aberdeen. On the north side it is within 3 miles of the river Don in a direct line, on the south side it is within 7 miles of the Dee. The length from east to west is fully 2¼ miles, the breadth from north to south is over 1 mile. The surrounding estates are: on the north, Carnaveron, Tillychetly, and Tonley; on the east, Tonley; on the south, Tillyfour; and on the west, Craigievar, the estates of Craigievar and Lynturk forming the whole of the parish of Leochel before its union with Cushnie. The

area of both estates is about 2200 acres, all of
which may be said to be either arable or under
wood, except a small piece of moss. The
elevation varies from under 600 ft. above sea-
level on the west along the Leochel burn, to
slightly over 1000 ft. on the top of the wooded
height south of the mansion-house. A fringe
of unreclaimed marshy ground at one time almost surrounded the estate of Lynturk ; but now,
except the small piece of moss between Upper
Farmton and Little Lynturk, the whole is arable
or under wood. The farms are : on the north,
Lower and Upper Farmton, and two at Little
Lynturk ; on the west, the farm and inn of Muggarthaugh, and Bridgend ; on the south, Clay-
mill, Drumdaig, and Buffle ; on the east, the
home farm of Lynturk. About half a mile south
of the mansion-house is the school of Lynturk,
endowed by the late Peter M'Combie, Esq. of
Lynturk. The handsome U.P. church and
manse, between Little Lynturk and Muggarthaugh, was built in place of the old church at

Buffle, where a Secession congregation existed
in the time of William M'Combie, the grandfather
of the present proprietor. There is also a blacksmith's shop and joiner's shop east and west of
Little Lynturk. The estate of Lynturk is surrounded by a good road, with branches where
necessary to the various farms. The greater part
of Lynturk is fine strong land, some of the land
on Bridgend so long farmed by Mr M'Combie
of Tillyfour being of exceptional fertility, Mr
M'Combie having reaped 13 quarters of oats
per acre one year off the southern slope of the
field on which the stackyard stands. There is
much fine wood on Lynturk, and a sawmill has
long existed in connection with the home farm.
A good deal of the home farm is in pasture,
there being an annual let of parks. As mentioned before, besides the modern mansion-house
—a plain two-storey building set in an amphithe-
atre of woods, plantations, and groups of fine
old trees—there is the house of Mr M'Combie's
grandfather, and another built on the site of the

old castle of Lynturk.   On the east side of
Lynturk, on the burn that, rising on the extreme
east of Tillyfour, flows between Lynturk and
Tonley for some distance, is a small but picturesque cascade known as the Linn of Lynturk,
in connection with which there is a traditionary
Lady of the Linn.[1]   Although there are many
fine views from various points on Lynturk, there
is nothing to compare with those from Easterskene, the wall of mountains encircling the vale of
Alford bounding the view almost on every side.

   Returning to the home farm of Easterskene,
we find that here, as at Lynturk, part of it is kept
in grass.   Several of these grass parks are let
annually, and have an unrivalled reputation for
the quality of the pasture.   One field which has
been over forty years in grass, situated in the
corner between the roads leading south and west
from the Kirkton of Skene, has been let at the
extraordinary rent of £9 per acre, which is believed to be the highest rent ever given in this
country for a grazing not in the immediate vicinity

[1] Appendix, Note T.

of a town, if indeed it has been equalled under any circumstances.

The home farm of Easterskene has for between forty and fifty years been the home of a herd of polled Aberdeen-Angus cattle, second in fame in Aberdeenshire only to that of Tillyfour. The Easterskene herd was founded in the beginning of the forties, a prize-winner at the Highland Society's show having been bred at Easterskene as early as 1845. Since then animals from the herd have gained the highest honours, time after time, at the Highland Society, the Royal Northern, and local Agricultural Societies' shows. The Easterskene herd has been conspicuous especially for the excellence of its bulls—Alaster the Second having beat the celebrated Fox Maule from Portlethen, that Mr M'Combie of Tillyfour declared to be "one of the best polled bulls ever exhibited." Caledonian II. and Taurus were Highland Society winners; and Paris II., after winning at the Royal Northern and Highland Society shows, was sold before he was two years old for 150 guineas. Mr M'Combie sent winners in the heifer classes at Highland Society's shows in 1869, 1873, and 1875, while Mr M'Combie of Tillyfour bought many prize-winners from Easterskene. So recently as December 1886, Mr M'Combie, with his Black Beauty of Easterskene heifer, bred and fed at Easterskene, obtained first prize in the polled cow or heifer class, and prize as Champion Scot both at Birmingham and London. The herd is as strong and flourishing as ever at the present time, and is the oldest established herd of note in Aberdeenshire.

In the management of the home farm of Easterskene, Mr M'Combie, in both farming and breeding, has shown an example that ought to be followed by every landed proprietor who has the welfare of his tenantry, and in a wider sense the good of his country, at heart. There is no attempt at a style of farming beyond a tenant's means, which can only discourage men of moderate capital. The bogs and heathery moors have been reclaimed by degrees at moderate cost. The fine crops grown at Easterskene are raised by means and processes within the reach of every intelligent enterprising farmer. The fine breeding herd has not been got together by buying right and left fancy animals at fancy prices, a method resorted to by many landed proprietors, who form herds not by their intelligence and skill as breeders, but by the length of their purses, a system generally beyond a tenant's means. The Easterskene herd has been formed from what was ordinary materials at first, by careful management, with the result that although fancy animals at fancy prices have gone out from Easterskene, few, if any, have been brought in; the method in this case being within a tenant's means, and the result of a nature to encourage a tenant to follow the method.

All this has been done under Mr M'Combie's own immediate superintendence. He knows, in much the same way as his tenants do, the trials, difficulties, fears, hopes, and rewards of the farmer's life. Farming with him has not been taken up in a spirit of *dilettanteism*, but has been an earnest practical pursuit.

If, as a practical farmer, Mr M'Combie has been an example to other landlords, much more has he been an example to be followed as a land-lord. No lawyer factor, a class who have been and are one of the greatest evils in the agricul-tural life of this country, not even a land-steward, comes between Mr M'Combie and his tenants. In the rare cases where a tenant and he cannot agree as to the value of a farm, an impartial arbiter is called in. The result is that only in very exceptional cases is there a change of tenant other than by succession. You look in vain in the newspapers for "eligible farms to let on the estates of Easterskene and Lynturk." Where, as in the case of Mr M'Combie, a landlord lives on his estates in the midst of his tenants, and knows the life of every tenant, as every tenant knows the life of his landlord, a feeling of mutual trust and friendship springs up, in which the unity of interest of landlord and tenant becomes a living present fact, at work all the year round, and not a remote abstract idea to be brought forth once a-year in after-dinner speeches at agricultural shows, and now and again at election times, or once or twice in a lifetime at marriage or coming-of-age rejoicings.

Country people see now and again, often at long intervals, a flag displayed from the top of the country seat of the *laird*, by which it is understood that he is there in person. This has for long been a "sign of the times," upon which much might be said, and which is having results in these latter days. If at Easterskene the display of a flag was made when the laird was absent for more than a day, the sight of the flag indicating his absence would be rarer than that indicating the presence of most others. While thus making his duties as a landlord the main business of his life, Mr M'Combie has given much of his time to public duties. He has been a Justice of the Peace for the long period of about sixty years, and is one of the only two remaining freeholders of the county, being enrolled as long ago as 1825. He was also for many years chairman of the parochial board of Skene, retiring only a year or two ago, much to the regret of every one on the board.

As was to be expected, the Volunteer movement received his hearty support.   Although when the movement originated he was about sixty years of age—a time of life when most people are thinking of retiring from active work—yet, when in his sixty-fifth year, he undertook the command of the 3d Aberdeenshire Rifle Volunteer Corps, and held the captaincy until 1870.   He was exceedingly popular with his men and brother officers, and when nearly seventy years of age stood as straight as any in the ranks, and was the tallest man in his company of nearly 100 volunteers.

In private life Mr M'Combie is highly esteemed as one of the most amiable and hearty of men, full of genial humour and wit.   His store of anecdotes, illustrative of the social life of Aberdeenshire in the end of last century and the beginning of the present, is unrivalled, and it is a great pity that a collection of these anecdotes has not been made for preservation, as many of them will soon be altogether lost, being known to few of the present generation even in the districts where they originated.   Mr M'Combie has all his

life been a great reader, and the collection of
books at Easterskene, especially those relating to
Scottish history, antiquities, and old lore in general, was declared by the late Mr Jervise, author
of the ' History of Angus and Mearns,' &c., who
occasionally visited at Easterskene, to be the best
private collection he knew of. Mr M'Combie is
an enthusiast in Scottish music, and an excellent
judge of it, and has a fine collection of old strath-
speys, many of them in MS., and very rare. He
loves to recall the powers of the late Mr James
Strachan, the famous Drumnagarrow, who used
to be the leading player at the Easterskene balls
many years ago. Mr M'Combie has all his life
been a stanch supporter of athletic sports, and
over twenty years ago capital games were held
at Lynturk and Muggarthaugh. For a good
many years past games have been held at Easterskene, where the leading athletes of the present
time, Donald Dinnie, George Davidson, and
Kenneth M'Crae, have appeared ; and we happen
to know that any of them, when opportunity offers,
would go to Easterskene in preference to most

places, if for nothing else than to show their respect for Mr M'Combie, as one who has so hearty
an appreciation of and interest in manly men and
manly sports.

In 1870, Mr M'Combie's popularity as a landlord and country gentleman received public recognition when he was entertained to dinner by
his Lynturk tenantry and the leading gentlemen
of the vale of Alford. The following account of
this dinner appeared in the 'Banffshire Journal'
of February 1, 1870: "The chief of the clan
M'Combie—the popular laird of Easterskene—
was entertained to dinner on the 21st ult. by the
tenantry on his estate of Lynturk, in the vale of
Alford. The chair was occupied by the laird's
cousin, Mr M'Combie, M.P. for West Aberdeenshire, who is tenant in Bridgend, the largest
farm on the Lynturk estate; and there was a
great gathering of the chief men of the vale.
The chairman referred to Mr M'Combie as a
kind and considerate landlord, who lets his farms
at moderate rents, who keeps no head of game,
and who lives among his people as an enter-

prising improver of the soil, and of the breeds
of cattle ; the winner of many a prize in the
show-yard ; as a warm supporter of the Volunteer
cause, having been for a lengthened period the
captain of the local volunteers ; and as a gentleman of the kindest heart and most agreeable
manners. In these observations the chairman
did not say a word more than was due to
Easterskene, and the large meeting cordially
endorsed the sentiments. The laird made a
suitable reply, and proposed the health of the
tenantry of Lynturk, coupled with Mr Hunter,
Farmton, who acknowledged." In addition to
the foregoing, Mr M'Combie has on more than
one occasion been entertained by his Easterskene
tenantry.

In politics Mr M'Combie is a Conservative of
a mild type, and were there more of the same
character, Conservatism would not be at so low
an ebb in Aberdeenshire. He has never, however, given much of his time nor attention to
politics, nor been an ardent party-man. Some
idea of Mr M'Combie personally has already

K

been given while mentioning his height. Until incapacitated from active outdoor exercise by an unfortunate accident some years ago, he might have been cited along with the late Mr Horatio Ross as an example of the remarkable preservation of strength in old age. When his portrait by Mr J. Coutts Michie was exhibited at Edinburgh in 1885, it was difficult to believe that the handsome, vigorous, and alert-looking old man was an octogenarian; and one critic thought doubtlessly that he showed remarkable critical acumen when he triumphantly asked, "Where are the wrinkles?" But the critic missed his mark, as critics sometimes do; for although now midway between eighty and ninety, Mr M'Combie's forehead is marked with only the faint outline of one or two wrinkles, just as the artist has faithfully delineated in the portrait.

In the difference between the condition of the estates of Easterskene and Lynturk at the present time, and their condition when Mr M'Combie entered into possession, lies the result of his life's work—a work the value of which is beyond all calculation. It rests there an accomplished fact, that has already borne much good fruit, and will continue, as all good work ever does, to bear fruit in a variety of ways and for a length of time beyond all human foresight.

In bringing our brief memoir to a close, we feel that in looking back to the solitary figure of Donald M‘Combie arriving poor and friendless in the vale of Alford some two hundred years ago, and then looking at the position of his descendant and representative of the present day, while enjoying his *otium cum dignitate* in a green old age as the respected and honoured proprietor of two fine estates, and the many other descendants who have brought respect and honour on the name of M‘Combie—such a retrospect cannot fail to be an incentive to individual effort in others, who may learn from it that prosperity always waits on energetic perseverance in well-doing, and invariably crowns it with success sooner or later. When, again, we compare the "life of sturt and strife" of John

M'Comie of Forter, with the peaceful career of his descendant at Easterskene, we see the advance the nation has made from revolution, imperfect civilisation, and lawlessness, to settled government, advanced civilisation, and conformity to law.

APPENDIX.

NOTE A, page 5.

"I OWN that John M'Intoshe of fforter, comonly called M'Comie, was a brave loyall gentleman, and behaved very worthily in the King's service. But he needs not be excepted in this place ; his predecessor, as he told me and others severall tymes, was a son of the House of Garvamore in Badenoch, where never a M'Intoshe treaded till this our age, otherwise than as a guest or passenger ; so was really Macphersone, as all the oy^r M'Intoshes in the south are, who tho by ane unacceptable mistake they bear yr name, have our nature, and constantly from age to age loved us better than them. But if he had been a M'Intoshe as he was called, he was neither at Glenclova nor at Blaire Castle, or the scidge of Lethen and Burgie, consequently that part of the history that concerns the services of the Catana tribus under the reign of King Charles the first, cannot at all be ascribed to the M'Intoshes, nor the rescue of Queen Mary, more than this, except that in contradiction to comon sence and reason, and the vouched testimonies of unexceptible witnesses, their bold assertion pass for a sufficient proofe."—From Sir Æneas M'Pherson[1] of Invereshie's MS. Memorial to the Laird of Cluny in Badenoch, *penes* M'Pherson of Cluny.

"The care taken by the family historians to record the natural offspring of William, seventh laird of M'Intosh, is sufficient proof that they were persons of note. The manners of the country and the time, both equally rude, may warrant the inference that the connection of which they were the issue was sanctioned by some such imperfect rite as that of handfasting. The mother of the two elder, Angus and Donald, appears to have been the daughter of the chief of the tribe of the M'Gillonies of Lochaber, a considerable branch of the Clan Cameron. The name of the mother of the three younger has not reached us; but from the marriage of her daughter to a person who was evidently of consequence, we may infer that she was of honourable rank. Both her sons seem to have received lands from their father, Sorald or

---

[1] The following notice of Sir Æneas M'Pherson is given in Douglas's 'Baronage of Scotland,' p. 360, ed. 1798: "Æneas, afterwards Sir Æneas, a man of great parts and learning, and highly esteemed both by King Charles II. and King James VII. He collected the materials for the history of the Clan M'Pherson, which is thought a valuable MS., is much esteemed, and is still preserved in the family. He was made Sheriff of Aberdeen by a charter under the great seal from King Charles II., dated 1684. His only son died a colonel in Spain, without issue." Sir Æneas was the second son of "William M'Pherson of Inneressie, who married Margaret, daughter of Farquhardson of Wardes" (Wardhouse in Aberdeenshire, which belonged to the Farquharsons of Invercauld). "His grandfather, Angus or Æneas M'Pherson of Inneressie, married a daughter of Farquharson of Bruickderg" (Broughdearg in Glenshee).

Sorlie ; and his descendants for two generations possessed lands apparently in the neighbourhood of Petty,
the favourite residence of their father. Of the elder,
the Latin History gives the following account: 'Adam
MacWilliam at first settled in Atholl, but afterwards
removed to Garvamore in Badenagh ; and from him are
descended the MacIntoshes of Glenshee, Strathairdle,
and Glenisla.' As his father died in 1368 at an advanced age, and as he was born before his father's
second marriage (of which there was issue), the date
of his birth may be placed in the middle of the fourteenth century (probably rather before than after
1350), and it is not likely that he long survived the
year 1400. Unless a further clue shall be discovered,
the endeavour to trace link by link the descent of the
MacIntoshes of Glenshee, Strathairdle, and Glenisla
from this common and remote progenitor, must be
abandoned as hopeless. [There is no record come down
to us of the particular Thomas M'Intosh from whom
the surname of M'Combie originated. The first mention of M'Thomas as surname seems to be in "Clan
Chattan's Band," Spalding Club Miscellany, vol. iv.
p. 260, where Aye M'Ane M'Thomas is mentioned.
Thomas as Christian name has always been kept up in
the family.—W. M'C. S.] It is, however, vouched in the
most direct manner by the family annalist, whose sources
of information and discriminating accuracy leave no
room for doubt in the matter. He is indeed to be re-
garded as so far a contemporary witness ; for of the
documents from which he compiled his work, it has
been seen that one was written within a century of the

death of Adam M'William, with whose children, at the farthest in the second generation, this eldest historian of the MacIntoshes (who was also the chief of the clan) must have been contemporary. The evidence thus far (that is, to about the year 1500) is unquestionable ; and by the other two historians, it is carried down in the same contemporary channel to the year 1550. The writer of the Latin History wrote shortly after the year 1679 ; so that the period as to which it was necessary for him to speak of his own knowledge is less than a century and a half, a period for which the amplest evidence of family descent is generally accessible even in the absence of written proofs, and among a people much less tenacious of such recollections than the Highlanders. It will be observed, also, that he speaks of the families of Glenshee, Strathairdle, and Glenisla as still existing, which gives additional weight to his evidence."—From ' Notes (MS.) on the Family of MacIntosh or M'Combie of Forthar in Glenisla, in the shire of Angus, descended from the Family of MacIntosh or of that Ilk, Captains of the Clan Chattan,' by the late Dr Joseph Robertson, the eminent antiquary, author of ' The Book of Bon Accord,' &c., written in 1839, *penes* Mr William M'Combie of Easterskene and Lynturk. In addition to the notes by Dr Robertson, the compiler desires to express his indebtedness to the exhaustive ' Historical Memoirs of the House and Clan of Mackintosh,' by Mr Alexander Mackintosh Shaw, for several interesting facts in the early history of the M'Combies.

NOTE B, page 5.

"To any one at all versant in matters of genealogy, it will be superfluous to remark that until a recent period[1] illegitimate birth was scarcely counted a spot in a pedigree. The instances are innumerable of lords, earls, and princes who subscribed and called themselves bastards; and there is scarcely a family in the peerage of Scotland in which, in some instance, the succession has not been carried on by an illegitimate son. In 1404, Alexander Stewart, a natural son of the Wolfe of Badenagh, acquired the Earldom of Mar, which he transmitted to *his natural son*, Sir Thomas Stewart." After citing other cases involving *damnatum coitum*, Mr Robertson quotes from Ferne's 'Blazon of Gentric, or Glorie of Generositie,' p. 287 (London, 1586): "Spurii qui ex damnato coitu procreantur, ita ut tempore procreationis, non possit esse matrimonium, omni prorsus beneficio excludantur." "It was," he continues, "perhaps scarcely necessary to cite these examples, for the history of the chiefs of the MacIntoshes itself furnishes a sufficient instance. In the beginning of the sixteenth century, on the occasion of a disputed succession to the chiefship, *the clan chose a bastard brother* of a late chief to be their captain."—Robertson, 'Notes on the Family of MacIntosh or M'Combie.' (See also Skene's 'Highlanders

---

[1] A writer, indeed, of the reign of King James VI. speaks thus of the practice of his day: "Observandum hodie et hoc est, quod bastardi, si a parentibus suis agnoscantur pro liberis nobilitatem ea parte patris recipiunt."—Craigii 'Jus Feudale,' lib. ii. § 21.

of Scotland,' vol. ii. p. 181; Sir Robert Gordon's 'General History of the Earldom of Sutherland,' p. 100.)

NOTE C, page 5.

"Hic Gulielmus erat supra communem popularem staturam procerus robustus sed minime camosus (?) ; eratque suæ familiæ primus qui Clan Chattanorum ducem subscripsit."—From 'De Origine et Incrumento Makintoshiorum Epitome.' The Latin History of the M'Intoshes, preserved in MS. in the Advocates' Library at Edinburgh.

NOTE D, page 6.

This was a feu-charter of the four-merk lands of Finnegand and shealing of Glenbeg, lying in Glenshee, in the barony of Middle Downie and sheriffdom of Perth, granted by Thomas Scott de Petgorno in favour of John M'Comy Moir ; Janet Rattray, his wife ; and their son and apparent heir, John M'Comy Moir, junior. Janet Rattray was a daughter of John Rattray of Dalrulzion, who was one of the witnesses. The charter also included "astrictis multuris omnium granorum prefatarum terrarum solitis et consuetis molendino meo de Innerreddertye," together with the long obsolete right of "*mulierum merchetis.*"

NOTE E, page 15.

The following extract from the records of the kirk-session of Kirkmichael (Perthshire) shows that the removal of M'Comie Mor from Finnegand had not taken place previous to 1651, and also throws considerable light on the Church discipline of the time: "March 2, 1651. — Ilk day Johne M'Intoishe of ffanneyzeand, Thomas Keill, and Alexr. M'Intoishe in Derrow, his tennants, maid public satisfaction in sackcloth, and gave (due) evidences of yr. repentances for deceiving the minister be causing him baptize ane chyld gottin in fornication, under the notione of a lawll. chyld."

NOTE F, page 36.

As still further showing the lawlessness of times comparatively not of a very remote date, the following incident, which took place before the time of M'Comie Mor, probably in Finla Mor's time, before the granting of the charter for Finnegand to the M'Comics, is of interest: " On another occasion, some Highlanders came down and killed a gentleman in Glenshee, one M'Omie or M'Homie. The Baron caught two of them, and instantly caused them to be hanged on birch-trees in the wood of Enochdhu. Their graves are to be seen there to this day. Their names were Donald-na-Slogg and Finlay-a-Baleia."—From 'Memoirs of the Family of Straloch, in Strathardle, commonly called Barron Reid (Robertson), written in 1728.'

NOTE G, page 36.

A most remarkable confirmation of this incident in M'Comic Mor's life took place not many years ago. A house was to be built on the part of the field where the caird was said to have been buried, and to the intense astonishment of those excavating the foundation, human bones were turned up which no one to whom the tradition was known doubted were those of the unfortunate caird. The event created a good deal of excitement at the time in Glenshee, and was looked upon as a most remarkable corroboration of a tradition which some, in the lapse of time, had begun to look upon with incredulity.

NOTE H, page 41.

Here, again, we would point out that none of the feats of strength attributed to M'Comic Mor are incredible, as so many traditionary feats are. Only a few years ago a celebrated athlete near Lochaber, in Inverness-shire, although at the time past his prime, on a bull attacking his brother, who was lame and unable to defend himself, at once rushed forward, seized the bull by his horns, and dislocated his neck.

NOTE I, page 47.

In a letter from the late William Shaw, Esq. of Milton of Blacklunans, to William M'Combie, Esq. of Easter-skene and Lynturk, written from Finnegand 26th February 1855, he says: " I promised to try and find out who your great forefather took prisoner in the north. James M'Intosh, one of the oldest men in our country, says that he has often heard that it was the laird of Craigievar, and *thinks* it was at the Kirkton of Alford the battle was fought. He does not know how he went there, only that Grahame (Montrose) and M'Comie were great friends. This was the more likely, as one of the lairds of Blacklunans, Robertson, Baron of the barony of Blacklunans, and one of Grahame's vassals, was with him. It was to this man that M'Comie showed his prisoner after the battle, asking him what he thought of him. The Baron said, ' Nae muckle.' M'Comie an-swered, ' Had you met him as I did, you would have another tale. Give him his sword, and he would drive all the lairds of Blackwater east Glack Pool,'[1] or the watery hollow, a pass between Blacklunans and Alyth." Now, in support of the above, we have, first, the testi-mony of " James Ramsay of Ogill," taken on 25th January 1645, and published in vol. ii. p. 167 of the

---

[1] There is reason to believe that what Mr Shaw calls the Glack Pool was the Glack of Fulzie, which is shown in a map in the possession of Mr Charles M'Kenzie of Borland, of date 1766, at the depression in the heights above Blacklunans through which the road to Alyth passed, and by which the routed lairds would flee in their imagined discomfiture by Craigievar.

'Memorials of Montrose and his Times,' printed for the
Maitland Club, 1850, from the original in the Montrose
charter-chest, that among those with Montrose at the
Law of Dundee, immediately after the battle of Tipper-
muir in 1644, was "John M'Colmy." Mr Shaw's infor-
mant was not sure where John M'Comie took his
prisoner, and it was at Aberdeen, not Alford, that
Craigievar was taken prisoner. Second, in 'The History
of the King's Majestie's Affaires in Scotland vnder the
Conduct of the Most Honourable James Marquess of
Montrose, in the years 1644, 1645, and 1646,' printed in
the year 1649, p. 49, it is stated : "They [Montrose's
forces] tooke prisoners one Forbes of Kragevar, a knight
of great esteeme with the enemy, and another, Forbes
of Boindle." Sir William, as we shall see, escaped.
Third, the evidence of Sir William Forbes of Craigievar, 25th January 1645, on which date "Sir William
Forbes of Craigievar, of the aidge of 32 years or therby,
marcit, being sworne and interrogait anent thoiss whome
he did see with the Erle Montroiss, Depones, that the
day of the conflict at Aberdein, the deponer being in
action and service for the weele of the Estaitts of this
Kingdome, he was taken prisoner upon the feilds be sum
of the Irish rebells and thair associatts, and wes deteand
prisoner be the space of a month, efter whiche tyme the
deponer wes permitted be the rebells to come aff upon
his paroill to returne agane, and that the deponer come
sua aff at Auldbar ; and that a twentie days or tharabout
therefter the deponer, for keeping of his paroll, went in
agane to the rebells at Strabogy ; and having stayed
two dayes or therabout he escaiped, and came aff at

Strabogy."—Maitland Club, 'Memorials of Montrose,', p. 167. We have therefore the fact that John M'Comie was with Montrose prior to his march and fight at Aberdeen, the tradition in Glenshee that he took prisoner the laird of Craigievar while with Montrose in the north, and the fact that Sir William Forbes of Craigievar was taken prisoner by some one in Montrose's army at Aberdeen, and may therefore safely conclude that Sir William Forbes had to succumb to the invincible M'Comie Mor.

NOTE J, page 47.

The complete list is as follows: "James, Erle of Montrose; Alexr. M'Donald, *alias* Colkittoches, sone; James, Erle of Airlie; Sr. Thomas and Sr. David Ogilvies, his sones; Jon. Stewart of Auchannachan; Donnald Glass M'Ronnald of Keppoche; David Graham of Gorthie; Patrik Graham, fiar of Inchbrakie; John M'Colmie; Donald Ro[ber]tsone, tutor of Strowan; Alexr. Ogilvie of Innerquharitie; John Stewart of Shierglass.

NOTE K, page 49.

Mr George M'Kenzie, John M'Comie's procurator in his law process with Lord Airlie, was also his leading counsel in the trial of 1673, by which time he was Sir George M'Kenzie. He was the son of Simon M'Kenzie of Lochslin, and was born in 1636. He early showed marked talent, and in the same year in which he appeared as counsel for John M'Comie against the Earl of Airlie, he was one of the counsel for the Marquis of Argyle. Dryden terms him "that noble wit of Scotland, Sir George M'Kenzie." Soon after the Restoration he was appointed a justice-depute. He was knighted before 1669, in which year he represented Ross in the Scottish Parliament. In 1677 he was appointed King's Advocate. One of his most distinguished public acts was the founding of the Advocates' Library of Edinburgh. He died in 1691.

NOTE L, page 54.

" From these proceedings it would appear that, firstly, John M'Intosh, otherwise M'Comie or M'Combie, held Forther in virtue of a contract of alienation (probably a wadset or redeemable right) made several years before 1661 ; secondly, that to the Glen of Glascorie or Camlochan he had acquired an absolute or irredeemable right, from the Earl having failed to redeem within the stipulated time ; thirdly, that M'Intosh was a person of very considerable note, influence, and wealth. Mention is made of his 'great power,' 'his moyen and favour,' with the English usurpers ; and again he is described as their partisan, or their 'intelligencer and favourite.' These expressions show that the person to whom they were applied was of no little importance ; and another incidental statement brings out his wealth. It is stated that in this disputed glen of Glascorie alone he had, besides divers horses, twenty milch kine and more than a hundred oxen.[1] The justice of the decision may certainly be suspected ; and it may be safely concluded that the 'Restoration Parliament,' as it was called, found little scruple in finding *for* a nobleman so eminent for his loyalty, and *against* a person who had been distinguished like M'Intosh as a 'favourite' of Cromwell's Government."—From 'Notes on the Family of MacIntosh or M'Combie of Forther,' by Dr Joseph Robertson.

NOTE M, page 58.

In the Decisions of the Lords of Council and Session from June 6, 1678, to July 30, 1712, vol. ii. p. 89, in a case, Logies against Wiseman, February 14, 1700, there occurs the following passage : "Transactions do not redintegrate null invalid deeds—8th December 1671, Mackintosh *contra* Spalden and Farquharson ; and 10th January 1677, Stuart *contra* Whiteford, where a son's bond given to liberate his father, unwarrantably detained, was found null." Here, M'Intosh against Spalding and Farquharson undoubtedly refers to the bond given by John M'Intosh, *alias* M'Comie's son or sons, for the liberation of their father in 1669. The Spalding is in all probability Spalding of Ashintully, fined in

---

[1] In a marginal note Dr Robertson adds : "John M'Intosh had in one glen more than 120 cattle. In 1574, the whole bestial which belonged to Sir Walter Scott of Branxholm, Knight (the ancestor of the noble house of Buccleuch), was 114 cattle—viz., 36 ky, 26 stottis, 21 queyis, 26 oxin, . 3 bullis, 2 stirkis—1397 sheep, and 841 hogs."

1673 for not appearing as a witness on behalf of the Farquharsons. Spalding had evidently received the bond as an equivalent for money from the Farquharsons, and found it valueless. The Farquharsons, therefore, did not profit even in a pecuniary sense by the abduction of John M'Comic.

NOTE N, page 76.

On the same day, "Andrew Spalding of Ashintullie; David Spalding, his brother; John Robertson of Tillimurdo; John M'Gillilvie, in Dalinamer; and David Rattray of Rannagullion," for not appearing as witnesses at the instance of the relict and nearest of kin of the deceased Robert Farquharson, were adjudged "to be in ane unlawe and amerciament of ane hundred merks Scotts."

NOTE O, page 77.

Robert Farquharson of Broughdearg's descent from Finla Mor is: Finla Mor, Lachlan Farquharson, William Farquharson, David Farquharson, Robert Farquharson. Alexander Farquharson, the son of Robert Farquharson who was slain at the Moss of Forfar, wrote what is known as the Broughdearg Manuscript, giving the genealogy of the Farquharsons. He was a surgeon, and practised about Bracmar. It is said that on being called on one occasion to prescribe for some woman related to the M'Comies, he said if he gave her anything it would be poison. The last male representative of the Farquharsons of Broughdearg was Thomas Farquharson of Baldovie, born 1770, died 1860. Robert Farquharson, besides his son Alexander, had a daughter, Margaret, married to John Smith in "Bredfald at Balgais"; also "a natural daughter, married to William Paton of Brewlands in Glenylla."—*Broughdearg MS.*

NOTE P, page 77.

While M'Comie Mor lived, the caterans gave the head of Glenisla a wide berth in their predatory incursions; and on his death, the one who brought the news home, on being asked, "What news?" joyfully replied in Gaelic, "News, and good news! Blessed be the Virgin Mary! the great M'Comie, in the head of the Lowlands, is dead, for as big and as strong as he was."

NOTE Q, page 83.

A fact which throws considerable light on the circumstances of the M'Comies subsequent to their father's death has recently come to light. In tracing back the history of the M'Kenzie family, who bought Finnegand in 1712, it appears that at one time the family was at Crandart, and afterwards in Glenbeg, and while in Glenbeg the head of the family lent money on the land of Crandart to a M'Intosh in 1687.

NOTE R, page 85.

Both in the Poll-book and on the gravestone the family name is spelled so as to pronounce M'Comie. In the Poll-book it is once M'Komy and once M'Comy. The *b* is a modern innovation, and was not introduced until about the end of the eighteenth century. After the time of Donald we have conformed to the modern usage, although etymologically it is incorrect.

NOTE S, page 123.

Another reminiscence of Mr M'Combie's youth carries us back to the time of Culloden. In 1818 there died a well-known man of the name of M'Bean, one of the class known as gentle beggars, at the great age of 102, whose death was chronicled at some length in the 'Aberdeen Journal' of that time. Mr M'Combie remembers having often talked with him about Culloden, where he charged with the M'Intoshes, who were fearfully cut up. M'Bean would have been about thirty years of age when he fought at Culloden.

NOTE T, page 136.

The Rev. Dr Taylor, in his account of the parish of Leochel-Cushnie, in the 'New Statistical Account of Scotland,' published in 1843, writing of the Linn, says:

"It is called the Linn of Lynturk, and has the reputation of being haunted by the apparition of a lady in
green or white ; but the oldest living inhabitant not
having had ocular demonstration, the colour of the
dress remains doubtful. The last instance of her appearance which tradition has handed down is the following : The laird of Kincraigie had dined with his
neighbour the laird of Tulloch, and as he returned
home late at night, mounted on a spirited horse, and
attended by a faithful dog, he was passing along the
brink of the dell above the Linn, when suddenly the
apparition seized the bridle of his horse, and exclaimed,
'Kincraigie Leslie, I've sought you long, but I've found
you now.' The dog, however, fiercely attacking the
spectre, it quitted the bridle for a moment, and the
horse dashed off at the top of his speed, while his ter-
rified master could see the spectre and the dog tumbling
down in mortal struggle to the very bottom of the dell.
Kincraigie was thus saved, and his generous canine
friend returned next day, showing evident marks of the
perilous strife in which he had been engaged."

ADDENDUM.

In the Dean of Lismore's 'Book of Gaelic Poetry,'
edited by the Rev. Thomas M'Lauchlan, there is a poem
by "The Baron Ewen M'Omie," on sickness. In a note
Mr M'Lauchlan says : "The editor has not been able to
identify the author of this poetical complaint. During
the existence of baronies, with their bailies or local

judges, the number of barons or baron bailies in the
Highlands must have been large. Of this class was
most likely our poet." Taking into consideration, first,
that the M'Omies were established as a separate branch
of the M'Intoshes, considerably anterior to the date of
the collection of these poems, and second, that the physician longed for is a M'Intosh, there is a strong probability that the writer was an ancestor of the present
M'Combies ; but the information is so indefinite as to
the time when and the place where the poem was composed, that it has been placed here as an interesting
addendum. The following is the English translation of
the poem, with the editor's notes :—

> " Long do I feel my lying here,
>   My health to me is a stranger ;
>   Fain would I pay my health's full price,
>   Were mine the numerous spoils.
>   A spoil of white-haired heavy cows,
>   A spoil of cows for drink or feasting.
>   I'd give besides the heavy bull,
>   If for my cure I had the price.
>   The herds and flocks of Mannanan,[1]
>   The sword and horn of MacCumhail,
>   The trumpet of Manallan[2] I'd give,
>   And the quiver Cuchullin,

---

[1] An ancient Celtic hero, from whom the Isle of Man takes its name,
as well as the district in Scotland called Slamannan.

[2] The editor has not been able to obtain any account of this person.
There is a contraction over the second *a* in the MS., which makes the
reading doubtful.

Ir, Evir, and Eireamon,[1]
And were I to possess them,
The harp of Curcheoil,[2] which hid men's grief,
The shield of the king of Golnor.[2]
Lomond's[3] ship of greatest fame,
Had I it upon the strand,
All I've seen I'd freely give,
Ere as now I'd long remain.
Long to me appears the coming
Of Alexander MacIntosh,
That my disease he might drive away,
And then I might no longer lie.

Long."

[1] The three sons of Milidh of Spain, from whom the Milesian races are descended, according to Celtic story.

[2] The editor can give no account of these names. The traditions respecting them seem to have perished.

[3] A famous Celtic hero, from whom Ben Lomond and Loch Lomond are said to derive their names.

THE END.

PRINTED BY WILLIAM BLACKWOOD AND SONS.

www.ingramcontent.com/pod-product-compliance
Lightning Source LLC
Chambersburg PA
CBHW030613040726
47497CB00008B/2962